PRAISE FOR
I HAVE NOT CONSIDERED CONSEQUENCES

"Such brightness and humor in these stories—they made me laugh and each one moved with its own joyful rhythm."

—Aimee Bender, author of *The Butterfly Lampshade*

"Sherrie Flick is an assassin. Book after book she has nimbly navigated the nighttime rooftops of our lives to sneak in and reveal to us our most private selves, and *I Have Not Considered Consequences* is her finest yet. This is electric, knife-sharp fiction that isn't afraid to bust open the armor and the costumes we wear every day. Just let go, trust this fierce, starlit voice."

—Paul Yoon, author of *The Hive and the Honey*

"'If she just cooked for him and unplugged everything, if they lived in complete silence, it would be fine. They would be happy forever.' Sherrie Flick's third collection of stories, *I Have Not Considered Consequences*, tests this premise with great wit and a big dollop of generosity. A wily bear, a sometime 'beartender' with piano-playing expertise whose brothers 'are all off in Alaska fishing' joyfully interrupts with his own luminescent stories. After all, 'who's going to second-guess a bear at happy hour?' Read it."

—Terese Svoboda, author of *The Long Swim*

"Sherrie Flick's *I Have Not Considered Consequences* reaffirms her mastery of the short story form. Her new collection is expansive in its scope, filled with quirky characters reconciling past with present, or present with future. In 'Chlorophyll and Oxidation,' the first-person narrator reflects on her past in Italy when 'the future is of no consequence,' and she reminisces with one of the men she traveled with those years ago when she was 'feral . . . I was a bear then.'"

—Linda Kass, founder and owner of Gramercy Books

ALSO BY SHERRIE FLICK

FICTION

Thank Your Lucky Stars: Short Stories
Whiskey, Etc.: Short (Short) Stories
Reconsidering Happiness: A Novel
I Call This Flirting: A Chapbook

NONFICTION

Homing: Instincts of a Rustbelt Feminist

COEDITOR

Flash Fiction America: 73 Very Short Stories
Best Small Fictions 2018

I HAVE NOT CONSIDERED CONSEQUENCES:
SHORT STORIES

I HAVE NOT CONSIDERED CONSEQUENCES

Short Stories

SHERRIE FLICK

Pittsburgh, PA

I Have Not Considered Consequences: Stories

Published by Autumn House Press

ISBN: 978-1-63768-104-6

Cover Art by David Pohl
Book Design by Kinsley Stocum
Author Photo by James Simon

Library of Congress Cataloging-in-Publication Data
Names: Flick, Sherrie, author.
Title: I have not considered consequences : short stories / Sherrie Flick.
Description: Pittsburgh, PA : Autumn House Press, 2025.
Identifiers: LCCN 2024059115 (print) | LCCN 2024059116 (ebook) | ISBN 9781637681046 (paperback) | ISBN 9781637681077 (epub)
Subjects: LCGFT: Flash fiction.
Classification: LCC PS3606.L533 I33 2025 (print) | LCC PS3606.L533 (ebook) | DDC 813/.6--dc23/eng/20241209
LC record available at https://lccn.loc.gov/2024059115
LC ebook record available at https://lccn.loc.gov/2024059116

Printed in the United States on acid-free paper that meets the international standards of permanent books intended for purchase by libraries.

Autumn House Press is a nonprofit corporation whose mission is the publication and promotion of poetry and other fine literature. The press gratefully acknowledges support from individual donors, public and private foundations, and government agencies. This book was supported, in part, by the Greater Pittsburgh Arts Council and the Pennsylvania Council on the Arts, a state agency funded by the Commonwealth of Pennsylvania.

For Rick

TABLE OF CONTENTS

I HAVE NOT CONSIDERED CONSEQUENCES

BREAKING

The bear holds his heart in his paws. Maybe he knows the heart is a symbol, even if it's a messy throbbing organ—warm in his paws, where it isn't supposed to be.

He offers it solemnly to Eliot. The bear's face relays a subtle motherfucker-did-you-see-*this?* expression. It reinforces the I'm-a-bear-holding-a-throbbing-heart-in-my-paws-in-the-middle-of-a-train-station-in-Budapest vibe.

Eliot, my housemate and friend, is aghast because he hates gooey things and also because hearts are complicated.

I personally understand that we're walking through the world oblivious to what's going on 99 percent of the time and then suddenly there's a bear in cotton undies—clean undies with flowers, butterflies, and green leafing vines, stretching across the bear's hairy ass—holding his thumping heart in his paws. The bear's ass is so big it seems infinite, yet the undies are just the right fit.

The bear seems anxious for Eliot to take the heart. But of course Eliot doesn't. He can't. Eliot is practical. "Too practical," he once admitted late at night, hanging out on our couch, his legs tucked up under him, gazing out the window as the TV blinked onto our faces. Too practical.

In my world? You grab the fucking heart. No questions asked. I would take the heart in a heartbeat. I can't wait to get my squishy fingers into it, feel its lush throbbing. I have not considered consequences, because I never do.

Eliot is nervous, shifting from foot to foot, ready to get back to the Eastern European itinerary he mapped out for us months ago. Our breath comes in frosty clouds and hovers over the platform of the train station, where we accidentally ran into the bear this morning.

It's a foggy Sunday morning in December 1991, in Budapest. The sky threatens snow, spits a few examples down at us. The bear's name is Reinhardt. He's from East Germany. Because it's 1991 and the world has just surprisingly, sledgehammeringly opened up into fissures that haven't quite settled into place yet, the bear looks guilty. The heart being a dead giveaway.

We try to help him. We suggest that he could maybe get a shopping bag for the heart. A box?

"I'll hold it for you," I say optimistically, holding out my mittened hands, which kind of look like paws, conveniently putting us on nearly even ground.

The bear looks at Eliot. Eliot shrugs. "She gets like this," he says.

I smile encouragingly. Pull my shoulders back a little. "I don't mind," I say. I'm young and invincible this morning, even with this head cold that's settled in.

The bear shifts from foot to foot in his cute undies. Both hands occupied. The icy fog crawls across the train tracks. The train station is otherworldly. A man walks by holding a live chicken, a string bag filled with cabbages strung across his back. The trains shift and spout like horses at the gate. I get distracted by their gritty grandeur.

When I turn back, Eliot is—against all odds—holding the sticky, pulsing heart. He has both hands extended away from his body. It looks like he thinks the heart might stain his clothes. He looks at the bear longingly. Later, he will blame me for all of this.

The bear, unburdened for the moment, rummages in his fur, his eyebrows furrowed, and pulls out a piece of worn paper. It has been folded and unfolded many times. I can feel the softness of the paper even before he pushes it toward me, into my mittens.

I pull off the mittens and hold the paper, gingerly open it to reveal sewing instructions for a simple blouse. A woman's face is sketched faintly over the instructions. Her face fills the page. She looks stern, competent, and very smart. Short hair, glasses.

I refold the paper.

Eliot thrusts the heart back to the bear, reluctantly wipes his hands on his jeans, looks around for—I'm guessing correctly—a bathroom, where he will work to disinfect his entire body. The bear rambles off, loping from side to side, his underwear slightly lopsided on his butt now. His heartbeat echoes throughout the station. He doesn't exactly seem lost, more like scheming how to get from point A to point B without getting caught holding his beating heart in his paws.

"Isn't he cold? Without a jacket?" Eliot asks.

"He's a bear," I say.

"But still," Eliot says.

I hand Eliot the paper, which he unfolds and stares at for a long time like it's a map of a familiar place, but the scale is all wrong. "It's you," Eliot says. "The drawing. It's of you. Didn't you recognize yourself? Do you know this bear?"

"We kissed on the train yesterday," I say. "He gave me some brandy for my cold, said I was beautiful. Just for fun. Kiss and done." I shrug.

"You're about to get us in trouble again, aren't you?" Eliot says. "Can we find an espresso and a bathroom before all hell breaks loose?"

Just then, on the other side of the tracks, we see two officers talking to the bear. The stern one, with a belted trench coat and high black boots, holds the heart out in front of him. The other one, in a short jacket with shiny black shoes, shakes his hand rapidly in front of the bear's snout, demanding papers that we all know Reinhardt does not have. Reinhardt shakes his head no and pulls off the underwear, flinging the stretchy cotton bundle onto the train tracks.

He says, "I'm a bear. A bear." His bear voice defies acoustics as he points to himself, turns to look at us, points his big bear paw to the train on the opposite tracks, faces the officers again, mumbling, mumbling. Shaking his head no, no, no. Eventually he walks onto the puffing train the officers have designated, head down, dragging his feet. Up the little stairs and the train door shuts and it's done—the last we see of him. Later on, we try to write him but nothing ever comes back in return.

The officer with the heart now wedged into his hat turns sharply, takes urgent strides in my direction. I make eye contact; his cold, beady eyes lock in. I reach out my hands, walk to meet him, to get what I deserve.

IN SEARCH OF

Helen could see one narrow chimney. Everything else remained covered by the fog that had lowered itself onto her town this bleak October morning. Around noon, it had lifted briefly and the stark detail of buildings re-emerged, but then the fog descended again, a tease, hiding the town from itself, the chimney Helen's only steady landmark. She wanted to wade out into the gray mist, but she'd promised Josh she'd wait for him to get home today. Josh, late as usual. But then his car turned into the driveway and she heard the mechanical clank and hum of the garage door opening and closing.

Helen listened for his footsteps in the mudroom. Sometimes Josh finished conversations in his car, droning work talk that he said he didn't want to bother her with, even though she secretly loved to hear these stories: Who won and who lost court cases. She liked being taken through the logic of it all, getting to the bottom of it.

Eventually the car door slammed with a muddled thud, and Josh's clunky shoes hit the short steps up to the mudroom and then through the kitchen. He didn't call up to her like usual. Instead he opened the refrigerator door, closed it. Opened some other kitchen drawers, mumbling to himself.

The act of waiting for Josh was an art form, a refined skill for Helen, even though it didn't seem like a skill to most people. She knew waiting for the right moment with Josh was as important as what she'd do when the moment arrived. Patient to a fault, her friends said. But really, what else could she do? She had spent so many years forming this version of herself. So much work getting herself up and out of her shitty little hometown and to New England for college so she could meet someone like Josh. Should she throw all of that out the window now just because Josh was late? Well, and maybe sometimes monotonous? No. She chose to stay stubbornly in love.

Josh thumped up the stairs to the sunroom, flopped into the chair opposite hers. As the gray started to lift again, Helen said, "It's too late, isn't it?" Josh looked out the window at the forms of buildings coming into focus.

"It's too late always, isn't it, dear?" he said. Josh fiddled with the wrapper to a granola bar, pulling at the crinkling plastic and cupping his hand under his chin to keep the crumbs contained.

Helen knew not to take Josh's bait. She practiced a kind of purposeful näiveté, ignoring Josh and moving toward her own private goals. "Want to go for a walk anyway?" she said.

The granola bar finished, Josh kicked off his shoes, wiggled his toes in his sock feet. "I don't know," he said. "My feet are sweaty and smelly and I just want to sit here for a few minutes."

The view had filled with detail now, a tugboat slowly plying the river. Helen leaned forward, and that leaning got her to standing. Soon she had shoes on and a light coat and without a word she opened and closed the front door—the door they never used except for company—and took off on foot into town. It felt nice not having to make conversation, to just take some time to notice the dented stop sign and the cracked sidewalks. To loiter. A word she'd always liked, bad connotations and all. What was better than loitering? And of course at her age, no one really cared where she stopped and started. She crossed Ash Street diagonally, heading toward the main street of the town. She felt a desire, a need to be in public, to walk quickly among strangers.

Until recently she had never really thought about her own mortality, but over the last few months it had settled like glitter at the bottom of a snow globe: friends dying, friends no longer willing to drive at night, friends forgetting they'd already told her the story of the missing avocado, twice. But Helen didn't feel old. She had finally gotten on with life, had just figured out how to be that confident and complete person she had envisioned at the start of adulthood.

Helen's shoe knocked a rock and she stumbled a bit but caught herself, no problem. Little shops had popped up on Main Street in the past few years, selling fancy candles, flavored olive oil, and weird T-shirts. A happy octopus holding cooking implements in its tentacles. A delightfully deranged rabbit with big round glasses, clutching a pint of beer. She personally didn't find the T-shirts that weird, but Josh did.

She paused in front of a new restaurant with a colorfully printed menu tacked to its bright blue door, and to her surprise, she opened that door and stepped in.

It was a tiny space, and she chose a two-top table against the wall. Most of the tables were two-tops, Helen noticed. She hung her coat on the other chair and settled herself by smoothing her skirt. *A nice early dinner*, she thought. Quietly, she thought, *fuck you, Josh*. A young man who had a grad-school look to him stepped up to her table. "Are you a grad student?" Helen said.

He blushed and said, "Is it that obvious?"

"I'm not sure why I said that out loud," Helen said. "I'm sure you don't look like a grad student to most people."

He laughed and said he was *such* a grad student, reading Edith Wharton for semesters on end. He knew it sounded stodgy. Maybe it was stodgy. He caught himself then and said, "Sparkling or flat?"

Helen chose sparkling because she always picked flat, and wondered out loud what she should order. She'd never been there before. Would he mind picking an appetizer and entrée for her? At this hour she was the restaurant's only patron and the waiter the only obvious employee. The dining room had the feel of an empty stage set. When he brought her the puréed carrot and shishito pepper app, he paused at the table, said, "Do you mind?" as he tapped the extra chair. Helen motioned to the open seat and nodded. He sat down and stretched out his long legs, revealing colorfully striped socks previously hidden by his black jeans and black shoes.

He introduced himself as Derrick. "I'm new here, studying at the university, but my sister owns a pretty high-end restaurant back in Kentucky where I used to work. I like waiting tables," he said. "Great money, and the whole clean, well-lighted place thing." Derrick swept his arm toward the empty tables. "It'll be packed here in an hour." He talked with the persistence of someone who had been alone too many days in a row. Helen understood the need to uncork and spill it all, to hear your voice out loud for a while.

She asked for the wine list. Ordered a petite Syrah. The tiny dining room was cozy with potted succulents at each table. Helen almost never ate by herself and never at a random place. Going out required planning these days. The idea of just wandering around and stopping in a place without Googling it first seemed completely new in how old it was.

"If you ever want a homecooked meal, I'm a good cook," Helen said. "You should come over." She immediately felt foolish offering up dinner to a stranger, wished she could take that back.

Derrick glanced at his little waiter notebook as if it held an answer. He nodded to himself, stood up. Helen sank down into her seat as he leaned in with a whisper. "You know, I might just take you up on that. Everyone in my program is so into sounding smart they don't say anything. It's eating away at my soul."

And so, Helen wrote down her address and phone number without much hesitation, finished her wine, left a big tip, and coated up. The prime-time dinner crowd trickled in as she slipped away, feeling liberated.

Helen liked being older now and knowing that people didn't see her as a walking, talking sexual object. She used to feel that way—a sexual drive coursing through her body that every man could see. What had she become? She didn't know, but it felt surprisingly powerful now that she didn't have to worry about Derrick the waiter taking her invite as a come-on. She didn't have to worry about telling Derrick about Josh. She didn't have to worry.

No one was more surprised than her when she and Derrick ended up in her bed the next Thursday, his day off from classes and work and Josh's day to meet up for mixed doubles at the indoor bubble court. It wasn't what she'd intended, of course, cooking a nice salmon with wild rice and a crisp romaine salad on the side. She had checked a couple Edith Wharton novels out of the library and thought they could break them down with a good discussion like she used to in college. Maybe Derrick could give her some unique insight into *The Buccaneers*. But then he reached for the pepper grinder and she leaned forward and somehow they kissed. It felt like an accident, a sliding of lips. She said, "I'm sorry," as if she'd burped.

Derrick laughed and said whoops and brushed at his face as if removing crumbs. "No worries," he said.

As they carried their empty plates to the kitchen, whatever had started back at the table edged along with them, and they made out by the sink, Helen instinctually reaching to turn off the hanging light. They slid down the hallway wall toward the bedroom. Helen's body clicked on its cruise control, electric. For a second, she had no idea how to stop herself. And then everything came back into focus in her head and body and the thrill dropped away like an anchor. They kissed some more on her bed, but the passion sputtered and they ended up propped side by side against the headboard, ankles crossed, talking about the xenophobic tropes in *Ethan Frome*.

"We should get up," Helen said. "This was weird, and exciting, but Josh will be home soon, and, even though we're fully clothed, it might be tricky to explain." Helen remembered times early on in their marriage when such exhilarating trysts ended differently, and anxiety hung in the air for weeks. Today, they both just laughed nervously, bounced off the bed, pulled the cover straight again, and plumped the pillows.

After they said goodbye at the door, shaking hands, Helen assumed she'd never see Derrick again. Soon she heard Josh's car turn into the garage. They stayed up late watching a show about dolphins, the TV light blinking into their faces, until they took the same path that she and Derrick had traveled earlier to the bedroom and curled themselves into sleep.

***

Edith Wharton was a stodgy woman. Everyone thought so. She was married to Teddy Wharton for twenty-seven unhappy years; there were rumors they never consummated the marriage. Teddy had affairs and then, a mental breakdown. Edith divorced him and just wrote and wrote and wrote—mostly excavating the suffocating, upper-class Victorian world around her.

In 1980, decades after her death, the public learned the details of Wharton's lusty affair with Morton Fullerton. She was forty-six when it started, in 1906. He was a young flirt, into men and women. It lasted three years.

"For sure, he'd fuck and run," Derrick told Helen, shrugging. "Including Wharton. It's how it goes sometimes, right?" He looked her in the eyes, clasped her free hand, the one that wasn't clutching *The House of Mirth*, and said, "I'm not Morton Fullerton."

Helen laughed. "I know you aren't," she said. "You aren't dark-haired or that kind of dashing, and we aren't fucking. Wait. Am I Edith Wharton?"

Derrick thought for a second and said, "Yeah. Kind of? Maybe." They both laughed and continued with their tiny book club, sitting fully clothed together under the covers of Derrick's futon bed in his chilly one-bedroom apartment, hacked out of an old, sagging Victorian on Walnut Street. Bright red flowers covered his fluffy duvet, a present from an ex-girlfriend, he said. Helen didn't know what she thought about any of this, but really—what was she doing? Nothing wrong. Sitting beside a grad student in his bed, under his covers, fully clothed, was alluring, sure, but technically not cheating. Though of course this rendezvous would have scandalized her if she was a character in a Wharton novel—alone in a bed with a man, *reading*.

The pleasant, tree-lined walk along the river to Derrick's place made Helen less lonely, so when he called a few days after the make-out dinner, she came bearing snacks and tea and a spare teapot she'd purchased on a long-ago trip to London. And then she did it again.

***

Edith Wharton was lonely too. Rich and smart and lonely. Like Helen, Edith had a strict and disapproving mother, but she lived in an elegant home in New York City—so fancy that, rumor had it, the phrase "Keeping up with the Joneses" started with her family: Edith's maiden name being Jones, her mother and father both coming from wealthy lines. But still, she was suffocated by the social mores of her time.

The silences in the passages of Wharton's novels drew Helen in. A kind of tension that surely came from Edith's childhood, but a repression that Helen herself had always associated with the working-class homes of her youth, where children needed to be quiet because some fathers worked second shift and lay wide-eyed behind a nearby bedroom door, curtains drawn, trying to sleep in the early afternoon.

Yes, Helen could remember the stillness of her own home, in her suffocating town. The slam of a cupboard, the noiselessness settling over the house like dust as she watched TV, as she played with her Barbie dolls. As she sighed and imagined herself stranded on a raft—out to sea with her stuffed animals.

***

Helen thought about Edith Wharton as she puttered around the house and attended her yoga class and her community volunteer meetings for the garden club. As she cross-country skied with Josh, she imagined Edith silently skiing beside her. *Why*, she thought. *Why the hell is Edith Wharton haunting me?* Sipping coffee in the café attached to the ski rental place, she heard herself ask Josh if they could visit Wharton's family home, The Mount, in Lenox. Josh rubbed his forehead like he did when he was irritated, but he said sure, okay, "Who's Edith Wharton? Let me check my calendar."

Getting Josh involved in the whole Wharton thing—her secret, sweet Derrick thing—was maybe a mistake. But they had been married a long time, and now she'd opened her mouth and Edith Wharton had come out, and so in the early spring, they took a short day trip to visit The Mount.

Josh found out that Edith played tennis, *lawn tennis*, as it were, and that she had learned archery and loved bicycling. Soon Helen found him reading *The Age of Innocence* after dinner in the living room. He suggested they stream the movie.

***

One drizzly day, she set out on foot to visit Derrick at work. She stopped in often enough now that people knew her face to say hello and welcome back. The bartender, the chef. She felt like she was part of something, and when Derrick seated her in his section, she told him about Josh reading Wharton. Derrick wondered aloud if he'd become some kind of literary guru, making Josh and Helen disciples. Helen laughed and thought *no*, but it did look a little absurd. What would Wharton have done? In between the awkward pauses, she would establish tension between the two men: one young, with great potential to succeed despite having the wrong breeding, and the other, handsomely graying and well-established, heralding from old money. Visiting cards and restrictive social rules and maybe a boat setting sail for Europe would resolve this silent tension. And of course the woman would lose standing in a way that devastated the rest of her life. Of course.

"You should come to dinner and meet Josh, I think," Helen said. More words she wanted to take back, but there was nothing to do now but roll with them. "It might be strange? But really, he's just a nice, boring guy who loves to talk about tennis and now, apparently, Edith Wharton."

Derrick hesitated. Darted to the kitchen for an order. Later, he snuck back to her table, tapped once on its edge. "You're sure?" he said. *Tap-tap.*

"Why not?" Helen said. "I mean, let's just see what happens, right? I think it's what Edith would do." Her cheeks flushed.

Derrick nodded. "Is that how we're making decisions these days? I have no idea where my dissertation is going, so why not add in my friend's tennis-loving husband?"

"Good," Helen said, sipping her Manhattan. She'd taken to ordering cocktails instead of wine, staying out the nights Josh worked late. She liked the raised coupe poised on its thin stem, slight condensation along its side, and the way the liquor glowed in the dim light. She liked the ritual of it. The burn of the whiskey at the back of her throat. Wharton had been a teetotaler and Helen thought that had really been a mistake, especially with a mother like hers. Some nights at the restaurant she could feel the liquor making room inside her—felt it giving her space apart from her mother, from the life she had fled for this settled one, a life that had opened Helen up even as it shut her down again.

Helen ordered a second cocktail, stayed for a little while to listen to the piano player who came on Thursdays, scurrying through the front door just minutes before his start time. He clutched his sheet music, stooped, head bent toward the piano bench, looking, Helen thought, very much like a squirrel. The piano player nodded to the bartender, mumbled a drink order, and then suddenly upright, back straight, hands poised above the keys, dug in. He started off playing swing and show tunes. Nodding, smiling to no one. Then the music turned toward slow, sad jazz, and soon Helen felt slow and sad. It was that easy. She tended to absorb the mood in a room, whatever it was, but especially melancholy. Helen wondered if everyone, every single person, tended toward sadness when given the prompt, just a little downhill shove.

She paid Derrick, tipped the shit out of him as usual, and waved as he strode to his next table, the restaurant abuzz with people she didn't know. People talking excitedly with cocktails in hand, trying to make room inside themselves for the idea of their own lives. She dropped some bills into the piano player's tip jar and he nodded to her as he dove back into his keys.

After she stepped into the street, the door closed and sucked away the restaurant chatter and music, leaving her on the sidewalk alone in the drizzle with her practical walking shoes. Helen headed home the long way around the park, not opening her umbrella, just letting the mist coat her face and hair. Tomorrow she'd tell Josh about the dinner plans unless she changed her mind. Maybe she'd make something Wharton would have served. A themed dinner. She'd invite a few people. She read somewhere that Wharton only held dinner parties for eight because only eight people in all of New York met her standards of conversation. Helen would limit her table to six. Their place was small, and she didn't want too many people to meet Derrick.

She told Josh about the dinner the next morning, about Derrick the grad-school scholar. About maybe inviting over the Randolphs to join? They liked books. Josh bustled himself out the door, a piece of dry toast stuck in his mouth. "Sure," he sputtered. "I'll call Johnny." The garage door rumbled, rumbled again, and Josh vanished into his world.

Derrick called soon thereafter. "I'm thinking of bringing someone," he said. Helen paused on the line, but then caught herself.

"Who?" she said.

"There's this Jane Austen scholar in my Edith Wharton seminar, and I keep thinking the two of you would really hit it off. So yeah, her—Rachel." Another long pause between them before he forged on. "She's petite, you'll hardly notice her." Derrick laughed. "Just kidding," he said. "She used to be a baker in another life and has promised to bring a killer dessert."

***

After searching around a little, Helen landed on a blog obsessed with both Wharton's fashion sense and her menus. She found a recipe for turkey stuffed with oysters with an oyster sauce, which seemed redundant, and a corn soufflé, which seemed pedestrian but who was Helen to judge? Wharton, she learned, sometimes waited an entire season to wear her newly acquired Parisian dresses in New York because American styles lagged so far behind.

Helen requested that everyone dress up a little and handprinted name cards for each plate. She didn't seat couples together, in order to (as the magazines said) stimulate conversation. She bought fresh flowers and stuffed them into a vase.

***

Derrick was right: Rachel was so petite it seemed Helen could easily stow her away in a carry-on. Adorable, with flawless skin. She barged through the front door, Derrick trailing behind. An alert young woman with tight-fitting, ankle-length plaid pants and an oversized white oxford and black lace-up shoes with no socks, she was made up of angles. A pixie cut. Dark-framed glasses. In a nod to the Victorian dress code, she had a sliver of silk scarf tied around her neck. Helen shook her hand. Rachel dove in, introducing herself to everyone and plucking an offered cocktail from Josh. Helen didn't not like her, but she did wish Rachel would stop talking for a moment.

"Yes, yes. What interests me most is that Austen embodies the historicity of the hysteric," Rachel said when asked about her studies. She looked forward at a distant horizon when she spoke, not at the people sipping cocktails around her.

Rachel had baked a luscious-looking orange pound cake with a chocolate glaze. "Austen would have eaten pound cake for breakfast, of course," she announced to the distant void in Helen's kitchen. "Her recipe would have also included a pound of each ingredient, but I've made this much more manageable, hopefully more delicious cake." She set the cake, centered elegantly on a glass plate, on Helen's countertop, twisting it a bit so it caught its light. She rubbed her small hands together, pushed her glasses up her nose, and smiled at Helen. A full eye contact smile. "Thank you for giving me an excuse to bake something. It absolutely made my day. Derrick just adores you, and I feel privileged to be invited to something outside the department."

Helen nodded, hands in oven mitts raised up like a surgeon. She wanted to press the mitts to the side of Rachel's face, but restrained herself. "So happy you could come," she said. "Everyone needs a little time off."

"Oh, I never stop thinking of Austen," Rachel said. "Although one thing I've found is that when I give research itself a break, it helps me understand her better. That's why I'm in the Wharton seminar with Derrick. Thinking about Jane through Edith." Rachel shook her head vehemently agreeing with herself. "My committee chair was against it, of course." She leaned toward Helen conspiratorially, and Helen automatically moved her head closer to Rachel's mouth, oven mitts still vertical. "No one knows I used to be a baker though," she said, holding up a single thin finger to make her point. "Only Derrick."

Rachel soon joined the rest of the guests in the living room, heading straight to the drink cart Josh had set up, not Victorian by any means, more midcentury *Dick Van Dyke Show*. Rachel sipped quickly at her second martini, chomped an olive, and then poured a big glass of water, drank that, and then went back to the martini.

Later, when Helen peeked out from the kitchen, Rachel was leaning against the wall beside Heather Randolph, a dear sweet children's librarian, who wore a vintage hat with a large feather blooming from its brim, arcing above her head. Heather's always-bright smile brightened even more when she caught Helen's eye. Rachel held a tiny pretzel aloft in her thin hand, nodding at Heather. "Austen is literally hysterical—conceptually, physically—and as a label hysterical, of course, is problematic on its own, as a feminist, as a woman, a human, but Austen is not historically literary and this is where my dissertation steps in." Helen decided she would slip Heather a shot of tequila next time she ventured out to check on the snack bowls.

***

They hadn't had a dinner party in so long. What had she and Josh been doing all these years? Had they encased themselves in Lucite, like bugs in a paperweight? Helen wasn't sure, but, maybe. She sometimes resented all the pressure that came with entertaining. The orchestrating of friends who might or might not get along when placed side by side with drinks. Right now, she needed to plate the turkey. Pull these soufflés out of their water bath and get people seated. But Derrick had already anticipated this step. With a kitchen towel draped theatrically over his arm, he pulled out chairs and placed plates. He sported a purple bow tie with his gray T-shirt and blazer. Everyone oohed and ahhed over the dishes, at Helen's effort at Whartonizing it all. Helen tapped her water glass with a knife, toasted friends new and old. Glasses clinked and clanged.

***

After dinner, Heather helped Helen with the dessert plates and the cake cutting. She pulled at Helen's elbow. "That poor sweet thing," she said. "She's just going to explode with all these Jane Austen masturbation ideas in her head."

Helen laughed. "I thought it was about hysteria?" she said. "I think it's her life's work." Heather nodded and Helen could immediately see her at the library's weekly story time, turning a page, smiling, reading about Sandra Boynton's vaguely competent hippo not going to the fair with the bear and the hare.

"Oh, she's intense," Heather said, grabbing two plates of cake. "But fun, in her way. A dear, really. Derrick is fun too. Where did you find these two? They're so serious." Heather said. She lowered her voice, touched Helen's wrist. "Are you sleeping with Derrick?"

"Ah no," Helen said, laughing, blushing, handing Heather a stack of dessert plates. "No. Why do you ask?" She shook her head, readjusted her apron. "Just sitting beside him on his bed mostly. I know it sounds ridiculous."

"Just wondered," Heather said, counting out clean forks. "It sounds anticlimactic."

"I met him through a series of spontaneous decisions," Helen said. Just as she started to explain the gray day, Josh being late, and the walk through town, the doorbell rang. No one ever rang their doorbell.

Derrick popped his head up from the table. "Oh," he said. "A surprise? I forgot to mention that I invited Trent."

"Trent?" Helen said.

"The piano player, from the restaurant? Squirrel guy?" he said. "Plot twist?"

There was a pounding on the front door, and Derrick scampered to open it. Trent leaned in, carrying his portable piano and stand, nodding, nodding. Josh nodded in time with him, patted his back. "Okay, then," Josh said. "Let's just set up the, um, piano over here." He rubbed his forehead, looked at Helen. Moved his drink cart.

***

After dinner, the party made its own grooves into its track, with the music sparkling up the room and more cocktails served and dessert done. Josh had trapped Rachel in a discussion at the table. "Serving," he said. "I know this isn't that interesting for you, but I think it applies to your studies. Serving, it's all power serving these days, guys hammering away from a mile behind the baseline. I long for the whole court player. Pete Sampras, Jim Courier, Ivan Lendl? Players."

Rachel nodded. "Okay, I don't know them," she said. "But Austen is the full court player in this scenario?"

"Right, yes," Josh said. "These days, players are so into *fitness*. Who wants a bodybuilder on the court? Not me. You?"

"Um, no," Rachel said. "Too much theory, not enough textual analysis."

"Right. We want bodybuilders in the gym and athletes on the court," Josh said.

"We might need another round of drinks in order for this to make more sense?" Rachel said, tipping her empty glass side to side.

"Yes, dear, excellent idea, in a minute," Josh said, pulling his chair a little closer to the table, pushing his jacket sleeves toward his elbows, moving her glass to the side, hands stretched wide. "I like to hit big. Who doesn't? But I think of my game as a meditation. A slow, unfolding meditation."

"Not sure who doesn't want to hit big," Rachel said. "We all want to publish, to win, to outdo the people who are trying to get there before us, sure." She nodded and smiled slyly at Josh.

***

Trent, wearing a bowler hat and suspenders, tapped away on his keyboard in the living room. Derrick settled himself onto the edge of the coffee table. "Edith read from her father's gentleman's library because she wasn't permitted to go to school. Just a governess to mainly teach her manners—that's all she got," he said to Johnny and Heather wedged into the couch.

"A governess is not nothing," Johnny said. His arm slung over Heather's shoulder, his cufflinks showing, his cummerbund puckered at his waist. Heather's hand rested on Johnny's knee.

"My theory is the deep memory of that lack of access changed her as she aged, though," Derrick said, both hands pointing toward them to make sure they followed. "I'm interested in age bias. In my dissertation I'll jump off Dawson's academic work, explore unequal privilege, how age is constructed and misunderstood, the modern preoccupation with it—and its ties to gendering, intergenerational conflicts. I want to take an intersectional look at how a contemporary Wharton would fare in a twenty-first-century literary landscape. That's where Helen comes in. She's sort of a case study for me." Derrick smiled at Helen, across the room, who before this hadn't considered herself a case study at all. She smiled back. Of course, she was a case study, obviously. It was obvious now, how Derrick's brain worked. How she was *theoretical.*

***

Josh had poured some coffee for himself, another drink for Rachel. He seemed at peace with tennis and Rachel and the party itself. They seemed to have come to a mutually satisfying conclusion regarding Judith Butler and new-style tennis racquets. Helen knew she should really clear the dessert plates. Instead, she poured herself a straight whiskey, plunked in a few slushy ice cubes from the bucket, felt a kind of lightness seep into her from somewhere beyond this room. *The world,* she thought, *is such a ridiculous place.*

"Tell me about your childhood, Rachel," Josh said, tapping the table for emphasis, spreading the linen tablecloth flat with his broad hands, picking at a few crumbs. "Delicious cake, by the way. I hear you used to be a baker?"

Helen settled into an overstuffed chair with a view of everyone, everything.

"Did you play sports? Did you have passions as a child?" Josh asked. "I'm very interested. Beyond Helen, my passion is tennis and it has served me well, no pun intended. It's also healthy exercise, healthy competition. You can play it your whole life. What did you do before this Austen came into your life? Before cakes?"

Rachel explained how her dreams of owning a bakery were dashed after the love of her life broke up with her and took her financing with him. Austen was her second-best passion, so she went with it. "I think my chair hates me though," she said. "I think she knows I'm not rooted in deep thinking, not committed on some cellular level. Like, you know, not bred in it. And it makes me think: Am I cut out for this? I feel so on the outside of everything."

Josh nodded, nodded, nodded. Helen knew he didn't necessarily agree or disagree with or even understand Rachel's point. Josh liked to hear people talk in long, long sentences. It calmed him. It made him return to tennis in his mind. The steady bounce of the ball on the court. The swing of his racquet, the contact, the power. The squeak of his shoes, the sweat, the glare of his opponent, the lob, the volley. A conversation materialized as the same thing as a relationship. Tension and release. Just keep it going. Keep it alive.

Helen sipped her drink, felt the shifting energies all around her. The music bopped and popped. She understood that whatever she said next could launch into action a series of events in this living room that would change her future entirely. She felt a fog lifting as she stood to join the conversation.

VITAMIN D

The bear takes vitamin D at night. It gives him crazy dreams. So crazy he's thankful when he opens his eyes. Outside his window, the gray skies drip with birds in compulsive flight south. "Go on," says the bear. "Go on, little dogies."

He imagines herding birds like cattle, the ever-changing geometric shapes of them. He closes his eyes, feels time ticking, weighting him to his sheets, pushing him into memories again.

Those photographs, all those boxes that read like evidence. He should get rid of them. Past lives, unfolding. He reaches out a paw, swipes the air. The same air those birds clamber through. *I'm on deadline*, the bear thinks.

It's the idea of coffee, its continuum of taste that drags him upright. A quick roll off the bed, paws to the floor.

"We start so slow," he mutters. "It takes forever for everything to get going." Water, filter, coffee, flame. The birds are already in their smart formation. Already, they're gone.

LIKE LOVE

Richard was one of the top marksmen on the University of Michigan's rifle team, 1972—clay pigeons and postal competitions. That all ended when he found himself sighting someone in from his dorm-room window one afternoon. He leveled his rifle, had the guy in his crosshairs.

He stopped himself—or someone came into the room. He says he can't remember which, but his hands started shaking that day and haven't stopped. He became an amateur photographer: nude, seminude shots of women, the camera firmly clamped into a tripod in his second-floor reading room. I imagine it's the same thrill as a big red bull's-eye, a fake bird, a deer, a man. He sights us up, coaxes our clothes off us. I don't know why I keep coming back here.

One time early on, Richard took me out to a barn in the dead of winter. A dirty, cracked window, some stairs leading to a loft, the smell of hay and ancient manure, misty light. He said he had an idea. He draped a fake fur coat across my shoulders. But he had forgotten his tripod and could only cup his unsteady hands around the hard metal camera like he was trying to save a baby bird. The photos all came out blurry. "Unsalvageable," he said, as he threw them into the garbage can.

At his house, I sit in his rocking chair, the one he made the summer he secluded himself in a cabin for months. That summer, it rained every day. He says he thought he was going crazy, listening to the sound of coyotes at night, high-pitched birdsong, and scrabbling chipmunks along the roof in the morning. So he made his idle hands busy. He sawed and sanded and fitted the chair into itself, forming it from vines and trees on the property using his dad's old tools.

In his youth, Richard was an Eagle Scout, and I can see it—in his posture and exacting side part, in his earnest, nerdy, unsuspecting looks. I can see him in a uniform, working steadily toward a badge, mastering the idea of self-sufficiency. Richard lives alone in this house, in this storybook town, where I also live for now, working as a waitress at the Pioneer Inn five days a week. He's my manager.

I sit in the rocking chair in his upstairs room on my days off. Of course, I recognize other waitresses' faces in the photos along his hallway. Richard scuttles in front of me, fiddling with speeds and apertures. The big, bright lights blare. The room is quiet and empty except for the chair and the camera.

He hands me a book, a heavy leatherbound thing, a present from his dead father. He moves his hands behind his back, nearly standing at attention. He says it's the only present his father ever gave him, and he doesn't understand why. I'm dressed in Richard's dark blue robe: thick terry cloth with a wide belt. My clothes—jeans, T-shirt, sneakers—are heaped in a pile in his bathroom. He wonders if I have something to say about the book. He says it seems like I should have something to say, because his father sure as fuck didn't. The pages are so soft as they flutter through my fingers. I do have things to say about how fragile everything is. Everything. But this isn't the time or place for such talk. I know that.

The robe is a big drowsy hug, and I drape my naked legs over the arm of the chair, rocking myself, absently turning the thin pages filled with romantic poetry from the seventeenth century.

In his office across the hall, Richard has a photograph of his ex-wife waist-deep in the ice-blue water of some gorge. The light is clear and cool. There are freckles scattered across her back. Her head turns, smiling, like she's in love. When I commented on the photo, Richard said, "If I'd just waited a couple more seconds for the light to shift."

When the late afternoon sun hits the corner of the room, Richard is ready. He asks me to stand, turn, drop the robe down my back. He asks me to look over my shoulder, not at the camera. Not at him. I drop the robe. The air rushes to meet my skin. I twist toward him with my arms crossed over my breasts. I'm glowing. I stare right into the camera's eye.

I know I could take a man like Richard and turn him inside out. Hit my target. I understand pulling a trigger. My hands tingle. The feeling starts at the tips of my fingers, circles my palms.

WINNING

Stuart adored fedoras. With a tiny feather, a hint of red, in the band. He favored three-piece suits and dress shoes, although he once wore Bermuda shorts and a white men's undershirt to a pool party. That day he felt naked, his pale legs exposed, feet laced up into white canvas sneakers like corsets. He clutched a glass of iced tea, stood at the far reaches of the fenced-in yard. Stuart declined the passed food but did sneak a piece of cold ham. He ate with his hand shielding his mouth like a little umbrella.

Stuart liked the walk to his neighborhood grocery store. Past the hedges lining the side of his property, which he tried to manage and then hired someone to trim, two blocks down the street, turn left. A small family-run place, it carried lots of Italian imports: sauce, olives, pasta. Little ornate tins of anchovies stacked into a tower. He walked to the store twice a week to shop for dinner, which he cooked for himself and his wife, Adele, and sometimes their Yorkie, Cooper.

Stuart let his face carry an air of amusement as he walked. Amused that he lived in this lesser midwestern city instead of New York or LA. Amused that he'd settled here, bought a house, married, and owned a dog with a pedigree. Somewhere along the way, he realized he'd fallen out and fallen in, simultaneously.

The front door of the grocery store swished open and Stuart's dress shoes swished in. A short stack of neatly wedged baskets greeted him. The store carried a fine assortment of vegetables, and Stuart often wondered who, besides himself, bought radicchio or broccoli rabe. He knew he would never meet these people, because he would never try to.

Stuart's personal claim to fame had come (with a quick burst of joy) when he first misnamed a vegetable the new checkout clerk had asked him to identify, thus getting an artichoke for the price of a cucumber. The puzzled, kind, but slightly agitated young person, intimidated by Stuart's permanent smirk and his weirdly timeless outfit, what with the hat and sometimes a long umbrella on days with no hint of rain, just wanted to finish ringing him up.

Stuart was a chronic liar. He lied and lied and lied, but this particular string of lies resulted in profit. Romanesco became iceberg lettuce, a pomegranate an apple. Sometimes he made up names like cutiebangbang for a kiwi, and the clerk put in a new code just for him, for it, the kiwi. Stuart hoarded his receipts, counted up his savings.

Stuart knew deep down inside himself a wounded thing thrived, a damaged part that made him do these things. All of them. It often felt like a rainstorm, rumbling inside of him, with his heart pounding. He'd been harmed by others. Wronged. Out in the day-to-day world, he subtly tried to hurt other people or showed them to be stupid in his own eyes, and this made him feel better.

The clerk rang up Stuart, thanked him for his help. Stuart grabbed his paper sack and crinkled it into the nook of his right arm. The doors of the store parted. Stuart walked the wide sidewalk back to his home, making up names for all the trees.

WE NEED TO TALK

The bear and I eventually, of course, dance in the street. The streetlights, spotlights. The smell of woodsmoke and pine. A misty fog. Me in a trench coat and heels. The bear, heavy and graceful, so poised and sturdy in his assurance. The pressure of a paw on my back, the slight push of the lead, the give of the follow. Hips, fur, feet.

SCOTTY, NOT SCOTT

The waiter's mustache curled up on each end. A handlebar, yes. As Ellie selected each course from that evening's menu, he made a face: a slow raise of the right side with her polenta-rapini choice, but a quick twitch from the left met the grilled radicchio decision. Her order, overall, leaned too bitter, he said.

Not convinced but also not, suddenly, wanting to disappoint the waiter, Ellie subbed in butternut squash soup for the salad. She wanted the Cynar mint-bourbon cocktail but Handlebar disagreed.

"No, no," he whispered and stomped his Doc-Martened foot just a little bit. If she really liked bourbon she would order the Stag cocktail, his personal favorite. "I can drink so many," he said, nodding, closing his eyes a bit. "I don't. But, I could."

He explained the Stag's bourbon forwardness, and she liked bourbon, yes? Yes, Ellie did like bourbon. She often drank more bourbon drinks than was acceptable, especially if she walked to the restaurant, which she had done this lovely spring evening—bird song dwindling, the smell of newly turned soil in the air. Again baffled that she seemed unwilling to disappoint this waiter and could no longer think for herself, she ordered the Stag and imagined a tiny horse galloping onto their table, balancing a shot glass on its back.

Her date, who by this time was showing obvious impatience to have his own choices assessed, said, "Hey, what about me?" He smiled at Handlebar.

The waiter smiled back. "Oh, you're next," he said, pointing a finger in his direction like a little pistol.

A blind date, rare for Ellie. What had she been thinking when she agreed to be set up by her extroverted office mate, Kevin? Ellie preferred eating alone at the bar. She also liked the cute bartender at this restaurant who, sure, was probably gay. She'd become a near-regular, but she didn't know the waitstaff because she preferred perching on a stool with her back to them all, chatting up the sweet, nonjudgmental bartender who made her the best Manhattans, each set gently on a napkin before her like a gift.

She had met her date outside the restaurant. They arrived simultaneously at the front door. In her past, this coincidence would have signaled an evening fated to go well, but Ellie was beyond such beliefs now. They were led to a four-top in the middle of the room, a small candle flickered between them on the slick wooden table. She hadn't noticed until now that the host had seated them beside someone she knew.

At first she couldn't place the guy, but then it came to her. Oh god. *Jack*. Jack, who Ellie had dated for a few months, many years ago. Jack, who now looked over at the order-and-assessment process going on at Ellie's table with a smug smile. The waiter had fallen into a stance with his feet more than shoulder width apart, like he'd trained for taking her date's order. Jack inched his hand up near his mouth and gave a wispy-fingered wave her way, mouthing hello, or maybe just hell.

Jack, also on some kind of a date, wore a tie and a nice blazer and sported a fancy, too-long beard, men's facial hair being all the rage this evening. Ellie raised her eyebrows at him and nodded solemnly. Jack had never worn nice clothes when they dated. She edged her chair toward her date, who sported a trimmed goatee, and all of whose desires had been approved by the waiter without comment.

"I know him," Ellie said, under her breath.

"The waiter?" her date said.

"No, no. The guy at the next table. Jack."

And her date—whose name was Scotty (not Scott)—took a look and said, too loudly, "Oh hey. Hi Jack, how you doing?" He pushed his chair back, stood up, and leaned over to the table, introducing himself with a hearty handshake. "I hear you know Ell? Cool."

Ellie saw it coming like a tornado touching the horizon as Jack opened his mouth. "Oh hey, Scotty" he said. "Why don't you join us?"

"Why not?" Scotty said.

This is how Ellie found herself at a table with a petite blonde massage therapist named Steph (not Stephanie) and Jack (former lover, good in bed, yes, but failed nonetheless) and Scotty (not Scott) who had already polished off one bread basket and now held the empty basket aloft, scanning the room for their waiter, who would surely advise against more bread before the first course.

Over in the far corner of the room, Ellie's favorite bartender diligently shook and stirred. His manicured mustache didn't seem forced on him. He didn't seem to care if it stayed or went. Head down, his cheeks rosy. Ellie wished she could join him.

"So," Scotty said, nodding at Ellie, "She good in bed?" And they all laughed, as if what he had said was funny.

BEAR IN A CANOE

The bear pushed at the canoe. It rocked, rocked, rocked, and finally went loose a little from the shore. He nudged it again and, empty, it floated out into the lake toward the setting sun. The bear considered for a moment that he'd done that all wrong. Oh well, the boat was gone, and he had other thoughts to think.

He waded belly deep into the crisp, clear water, and little fish plucked at his fur as the sun turned otherworldly yellow, orange, pink. Soon, the small heat of the light came across to him in little waves lapping. The bear closed his eyes to take it all in. The boat was floating far from shore now. It surely belonged to someone who would miss it, and who would blame someone else for letting it go missing. Of this the bear was certain.

Eventually the sun sank, a big leaden orange ball by the end of its show. Evening passed and the moon rose, cold and bright. The lake air turned misty, moonlight casting everything silver. Geese honked and splattered into the water. The herons, who earlier tip-toed through the rocks with such grace, now squawked from their nests in the marsh. The bear wondered how long any of this could last. He saw the slick oil in the water from the trolling motors. The abandoned fishing lures. The water levels weren't what his father knew. The bear had been thinking about this lately. Endings.

The bear could see the boat had now floated back toward shore farther up along the tree-lined bank. He lumbered in that direction, through the shallows. The moon slowed everything down, including his own heart—or it seemed that way. The crickets and cicadas started up, and swarms of mosquitoes tightly orbited the bear's head like an electric hairnet. The bear clawed a few times, swatted. The swarm rose and fell as he made his way toward the canoe.

As he followed the shoreline, the lights of the campers and cabins nestled back in the woods shone through the trees. He knew the circuit well. He tipped garbage cans here, and sometimes the extra special cooler that a drunken party left outside. He couldn't help himself as he helped himself. He always left a mess. Styrofoam, glass, half-eaten sandwiches and apples.

Now the frogs popped and croaked. Stars pinpricked themselves to the sky one by one as the bear neared the boat, snagged now on a snapped tree limb. The bear had noticed more trees tipping these past couple years, lifted up, their root skirts exposed to the water.

Green and wide at the center, the canoe looked like a giant turtle. The bear pushed at it again. It wobbled in the flat water, made concentric ripples away from him. The lake fell silent and still. It was nice this time of night, no motorboats or the splash of kids diving through innertubes.

The bear grabbed the little rope on the front of the canoe with his big paw and pulled it to shore. Once on land, he shook until his fur felt puffed. He sat down on the small sandy beach to think a little about the why of it all.

Eventually, the bear got his gumption up, shoved and flopped himself into the boat. It almost capsized, but the bear steadied it, and then he drifted out into the lake, seated in the canoe. He swiveled his head to scan the shoreline that encircled him like an old friend, the moonlight vibrating down. He pushed at the water with his thick paws. The bear lay back, feet up on one seat, his head resting on the other, and let the boat gently rock him.

He could see the future coming. He imagined all the water gone and him still at the lake's center in this canoe, slumped on rocks and mud. Someday soon, he knew, he'd be pushed somewhere that didn't make sense.

But tonight, the canoe rocked him into being a thankful bear. He heard the swish and plop of a fish nearby. *Breakfast*, he thought, as he fell asleep. By morning, the boat would be nestled into a bramble of berries, the bear out and up the bank, lumbering away.

LIVING

Marko ran twelve miles. The photo he posts shows a rocky trail and bright morning sky. I ate a blueberry muffin while standing over the sink. Marko asked his boss if he could give two presentations to the board instead of one because he loves to prep difficult calculations. Photo of a spreadsheet. I walked my dog exactly .38 miles and swept the kitchen floor. Marko has lost twenty-five pounds without even trying. Photo of his naked, flat stomach. I lost my cell phone but then found it again and then took a nap. Marko posts a beautiful but not too beautiful photo of himself and his wife, both drinking local hoppy beers with ironic names, smiling into the selfie lens. My boyfriend broke up with me, but I'm still seeing him so I haven't told anyone we broke up; sometimes he shows up at my house unannounced and wants to have sex, and I want to have sex, but then we have sex and I say, what's up and he says, I don't have time for a commitment anymore. Marko enjoys a pour-over. I walk through the park, taking the longest trail. I wander, not walking for exercise. I wonder if this is how my life will advance—I'll have these nearly imaginary social media friends living these dynamic lives, and I'll just wipe down the kitchen sink really well. Marko receives an award that I am positive he deserves. Photo of Marko with a medal around his neck. I post photos of birds that come to my feeder. One after another, blurry bird photos that get four or five sympathy likes. Marko posts a photo of a cool owl he saw on his midnight marathon training run and gets 500 likes in three minutes. I don't know 500 people, pretty sure. I used to know Marko a long time ago. Never my boyfriend but sometimes my almost-boyfriend in that way groups of friends kind of never know what's going on or who wants who. Marko played drums in high school and also in a side band called Breakneck. A bit stiff for a drummer, but very exacting. He had immaculate posture and one time definitely went out with my friend Tawnya. They walked together at the carnival and he threw darts to win her a mirror with the band Rush's logo painted on it. Styx, Rush, Lynyrd Skynyrd, Led Zepplin. These bands seem like ancient oracles now. Marko moved away to Rhode Island and married the wife whose picture he posts with the beer he drinks, and they both amble forward toward so much seemingly accidental success with somehow more hours in the day than other people have in their days. I have twenty-four hours in my day. Every day. For sure.

Then one day Marko posts a photo with his dog and a woman who is not his wife, but who he calls his wife, and announces, without explanation: FIRST THANKSGIVING TOGETHER! I had Thanksgiving with my four friends. We ate all the regular stuff and too much of it and then lay around on couches just watching TV with no drama whatsoever between us.

Marko's flawless life continues but it's definitely a different woman in the photos. A new wife, and they seem to be training border collies too. That's new. Marko has read seventy-five books so far this year and that makes me wonder if he has any friends at all. I've read ten books, but I also drank too many margaritas with my four friends on Tuesday night. I also ate some delicious french fries. Back in the day, Marko walked stiffly and even though he was a drummer, he became a Republican. He continues being a music guy and also a conservative, smiling, confident-in-trickle-down-theory political guy and there is no conflict in that or anything else he does—except for that wife swap. But even that was smooth and successful, and what happened to the old wife? All those pictures suddenly disappeared. Gone. Revised. The first wife too proud to unfriend Marko, because she doesn't want to give anyone the wrong idea. I repost a photo of that wife looking happy, squinting into the sun at opening day for the farmers' market, Marko's arm slung over her shoulder while holding a canvas tote, a photo I screenshotted ages ago. I do this just to keep everyone honest, just to imagine Marko's finger hovering above it, almost clicking that little heart.

CHLOROPHYLL AND OXIDATION

I'm in my kitchen, but also in Italy, 1991. Back there, I sit on a folding chair, unfolded in front of crumbling walls, perfect light. Here, a magical Bluetooth speaker plays Fleetwood Mac. I wear practical socks. They're red; my friend Brian recommended them. They gently squeeze my calves.

There, I sit cross-legged. I am wearing two sweaters, a scarf, tights, and a long skirt. Winter in Rome? Florence? Pompeii? Venice? I'll soon have sex. Am always wanting to have sex. More than any lover does, even, and I am, possibly, intimidating because of my lust's surging power.

Here, I light some candles, sit in a leather chair in the corner. I'm surrounded by plants. I thought my life might turn out this way, actually. There, the future is of no consequence. There, I always want to go away, to escape—myself, the lust—but I don't have a great sense of direction, so someone steps in to navigate and that someone is usually a man.

I have this need instinctually—to leave, to go, to get lost. Beyond these decisions, the world continues to spin. Boundaries all around that I can't see. Gravity and humidity and the laws of thermodynamics. So many invisible rules.

Chlorophyll and oxidation.

Now I call up one of the men I traveled with all those years ago, Eliot, a housemate I never slept with. We reminisce about it all. The mistakes we made. Our disregard for the future, for consequences. We should have lived together forever, we both say. Single and happy in a city, we say. "But I was feral then," I say. "I was a bear then, remember?"

Look at me here in the chair in the photo—you can't tell now, but it's true.

"I was practical," he says. "Too practical."

"I should've been bossier," I say. He agrees.

We both laugh.

Eventually, we both cry a little. "I'm melancholy, not sad," he says. I don't understand the difference, but I'm pretty sure I'm sad, not melancholy.

But I must get off the phone. I've made homemade paneer. Two stacked cast iron skillets, threatening to topple, press the fresh cheese into a round.

It reminds me of eating palak paneer for the first time in London. So spicy I could barely breathe, and when I abandoned the leftovers I'd carted home on the counter, the eccentric white cat that came with the flat ate them without batting an eye.

I'm freefalling through time again. What happened to that cat? Why did I think I had to stop seducing all those men? Everyone told me to. Everyone. Mary Lou, another friend from long ago, once scolded: "In the future, I see you running after a man, almost catching up, touching the edge of his coat. The man doesn't have a face. Forever."

I decided I didn't want that. I decided I wasn't weak.

But still, it takes a while these days to return to the here and now. Being lost in my head isn't much worse than being lost in Prague, that time near the train station. My lover had bought me a single white flower that I had to leave behind in the hotel room, because flowers and backpacks don't mix. I have nothing tangible from him, except this photograph from Italy, where I'm young and in charge, with my big bear heart pounding in place. I'm ready to unfold from the chair. Ready to walk away and dance.

LOST IN TIME

"You know, though—that's fish. They either die the first day or live for a decade," Matty said as he swiftly scooped Patti Smith out of the aquarium.

The fish, which had squiggled in its plastic bag yesterday and zoomed around the aquarium that morning like a rocket ship, gave no resistance in the net. Squishy dead. Gone. Matty had named her Patti Smith, and although a person had to work to get close to a fish (it wasn't like a puppy or a kitten), they'd both really liked Patti from the get-go, her little neon stripe, her diligent swimming.

Matty, a practical guy, thumped the net on the toilet seat and watched the fish plop into the bowl. "Bye-bye," he said, then flushed, and washed his hands.

Trudy wished Matty had more empathy when dealing with this kind of thing. Matty thought Trudy cried too easily, and that was true, too. She cried during the opening credits of movies and she cried when a little kid picked up a crunchy leaf off the sidewalk and handed it to their mom. She also cried, apparently, when a fish named after one of her favorite singers died. Slow, soft weeping, barely noticeable to those who didn't know her well. Trudy hadn't always been like this, her emotions leaking out all over the place. But then the world had shut down and opened up, and then revised itself to be unrecognizable, while also sort of staying the same.

Matty smacked his thick hands together, dried them on a towel, and said, "Okay, let's do it!"

"Do what?" Trudy said, moving to the couch, grabbing a big yellow throw pillow for her lap. "Go out after Patti Smith just died?"

"Look at Kurt Cobain and Bob Mould," Matty said. "They're both in there, still swimming around. They've been around forever. C'mon, you don't even care about the aquarium, Trudy. Let's go get some wings and play pinball."

That was the plan. Kind of a retro mid-90s, mid-week date. A date-date. They'd cut loose for an entire night, no bitching about work. They could talk about bands and books and TV shows they liked. They'd leave their phones on the kitchen counter. They'd laugh at themselves, be both cynical and ironic. Maybe they'd even buy a pack of cigarettes and smoke, huddled outside on the sidewalk.

Trudy pushed at the pillow; its puffy insides gave way, bounced back, gave way, bounced back. She teared up a little again. "I don't know, Matty. I don't think I can do it tonight."

Matty stiffly set his coat on a bar stool, moved behind the kitchen island and held his tumbler under the fridge's button for water. It made a quick hissing sound and the glass filled. Trudy knew he drank water to distract himself from saying something that would upset her. He filled a second glass. "We really need to get out of this house, Trudy. I mean, we can't work here full time and then spend our free time here. It isn't healthy," Matty said, looking at the ceiling, a hand wedged into his curly, always chaotic hair. "The walls are closing in. I need some surprises in my life. I'm bored. Bored."

Trudy put up a hand like a stop sign. "No, we don't get to talk about your boredom this evening. I did not cause a global pandemic. I did not invent Zoom. I cannot talk this through again. Can. Not. No." She squeezed the pillow one more time and then walked to wash her face and get her coat from the closet. She found her most stylish shoes in their bedroom. She zipped and tied up. Grabbed the keys and walked out the door without a word. She stood in the hallway until Matty joined her.

"Jesus," he said. He closed the door and made sure the handle latched.

They put on masks because it was still a building policy, got into the elevator, rode two floors down, pushed at the front doors, and walked into the cold damp night, tucking the masks back into their jacket pockets.

They'd heard about this new place with duck pin bowling and

pinball machines, so they walked in that direction. The place had once been a movie theater. "Excellent, who goes to movies anymore, anyway?" Matty said when he found out about the transformation. But Trudy loved going to movies. In her twenties, she attended matinees, double features, art house films, blockbusters. It didn't matter. Settling into the cushy seat, digging through her popcorn bag. She loved watching movies by herself, but that was before she'd met Matty. So she said, "Yeah, fuck movies."

The place had a neon sign out front and a list of pinball games where the marquee for the films used to be. "Oh, *The Munsters*," Matty said. "I used to totally kick ass on that after a double at Doogie's."

The evening felt like an audition for a throwback movie, with Trudy poorly reciting lines she had once known by heart. How could she be a convincing slacker with a savings account and an IRA, nice pots and pans, a chiropractor, houseplants. A giant fish tank, for Christ's sake.

***

The building smelled like electronics, the same smell that once wafted out of the arcade in Trudy's hometown mall. It made her heart pitter-patter. She loved the grease and the wires behind it all. The mechanics. It was so much better than AI or code. *Fuck Zoom*, she thought.

They tapped a credit card for tokens. Trudy wanted to venture off on her own like she used to at the bars, but because it was "date night" they played pinball at the same machine. They found *The Munsters* and got some extra balls and the lights flashed. They high-fived when they matched, the hammer inside the machine announcing a free game.

Holding the machine like a bucking bronco, trying to score and not tilt while still looking calm and cool, could really reset a person. It felt sexy. Or at least reminded Trudy of a sexier time in her life. They played a couple of games on *Fish Tales* in honor of Patti Smith and got the giant rubber fish to flop around when they scored big. Then they moved on to *Attack from Mars* and *The Addams Family*, which featured Thing, the creepy rubber hand that rose up from a box and grabbed the ball and took it back to the pinball dungeon. *Twilight Zone* and *Creature from the Black Lagoon*. Guns N' Roses and The Who's

Tommy blasted through shitty pinball speakers. It was all there. *Galaga* and *Pac-Man* and *Tetris*. All of it. They both still had the touch.

They drank pint glasses of a local pale ale at the almost empty bar and followed each other from machine to machine. There was nearly no one to check out in the downtime—a few twenty-somethings slouched at the far end of the room with the look of the eternally cool. Dressed in black with skinny jeans hugging their skinny frames, Converse sneakers, leather jackets, and wallet chains sneaking across their hips. They were pretty good at their machine though. *Police Force*. Free games popped, lights blinked, a siren wailed, bullets rat-tat-tatted. Their expressions never changed below their spikey, dyed-black hair. A masked worker walked the floor, disinfectant spray bottle in hand, a wipe in the other, rubbing down the plungers and flipper buttons, sweeping up loose candy wrappers and discarded plastic straws. A tap on the arm, and it was Trudy's turn again. She pressed start twice and plunged the ball into outer space.

***

Walking home, Trudy and Matty held hands. Their arms buzzed from two hours of pinball play, and they felt a bit sensory overloaded, but good, more alive. The weather had turned misty. It slicked up their faces and hair, making them glow in the streetlights. It reminded Trudy of the one gig her band, The Lickers, got to play in London. A complete fluke.

"You didn't know me in the '90s," Trudy said. "I never cried then. Never."

Matty kicked a stone along the sidewalk ahead of them, doing a big wind-up with his loafer. "That doesn't surprise me. I can tell you've softened from something you used to be. Probably best for me to have this version."

Trudy laughed. "Probably. I was a lot to handle then. I had big dreams. My band always on the verge of making it. At one point I truly believed The Lickers would tour and release albums, and I'd live the 3 a.m. life of thrift store dresses, sleeping on friends' couches, whiskey, and cocaine, forever. It's all such a cliché now," Trudy said. "So embarrassing." She let go of Matty's hand, stuffed hers into her coat pockets. Took a deep breath. "Fuck, man. I am old." Then she laughed and Matty laughed and they decided to stop at a little café that stayed open late and drink some cocktails.

They ordered pommes frites with gravy. Trudy talked about the silky sound quality of vinyl versus shitty CDs, forget streaming. The visual superiority of handmade band signs plastered up with wheat paste. Matty talked about how Raymond Carver's stories changed his life. "That community college class? That professor had no idea. All those silences, all that drinking? I was right there with Carver's characters, with him," he said, clasping his hands together above his lowball glass. "I decided, what the hell. I'd just keep reading and writing papers until I got a degree. Who knew an English Lit degree would lead me to a seedy, successful job in finance?"

"Selling out," Trudy said, tipping her cocktail glass against his. "It was bound to happen. Not sustainable, that life. Who knew *content* would become so marketable? Hey, we tried not to make it." They both took long sips, basked in the tiny candlelight of their table.

"If I hadn't decided to take that Post Modernism seminar, I never would have met you, Trudy," Matty said. "I don't know what I would have done if I'd never met you." His dark eyes held even with hers. He brushed her cheek with his hand, cupped the side of her head. Trudy felt like she was looking at him for the first time in years.

When they returned to their condo, masks on, masks off, rubbing their shoes on the hemp welcome mat in the hallway, taking them off so they didn't get their white carpet dirty, after the keys jangled them inside, their eyes landed on the aquarium against the far wall. Trudy was sure Kurt Cobain and Bob Mould would be belly-up, glassy-eyed, and gone, but they weren't. They swam nonchalantly around their little castle and nibbled at the flakes Matty crumbled onto the water's surface.

"An aquarium is a commitment," Matty said to the bubbling water. The date had made him feel like he was somehow haunting himself. There was a time when he didn't want anything more than to be an intellectual bartender—drinking, going to shows, playing eight ball. He figured he was a lifer, like Dan-Dan and Scott, who'd been at Doogie's since it opened in the '80s. Flirting with women, pouring shots, cutting off the people who'd made it onto The List, waking up at 2 p.m. after a closing shift with one of the women he'd flirted with the night before. And then doing it all over again.

Matty's former self would have killed everything in this tank. Instead, it had pretty aquatic plants and clean gravel and an evenly flowing pump and all the other fish in addition to his two favorites, plus a few snails to work on the algae. It was a commitment. And Matty was a competent guy, making good money. A little overweight, a little bored, but stable. Some days he longed for the old days the same way he longed for a cigarette. But he'd kicked those ages ago.

He snapped the fish food container closed. Nestled it in its tray. "It's weird I never saw your band," Matty said to Trudy, who was now sprawled out on the sectional, feet propped up on the yellow pillow. She popped her head up like an otter.

"The Lickers? Oh, we were obscure and short-lived."

"Yeah, but I saw a lot of bands back in those days," he said, joining her. "Quality did not matter." He laughed, rubbing Trudy's toes, her arch, the two tender spots on each side of her heel. "I dunno. It would have been cool if I'd seen you and your band then but didn't know you and then we met and found out years later."

Trudy's eyes closed. "Probably better that you didn't. You would've been like, 'Oh that's that singer who puked on stage and forgot the lyrics to the third verse and instead just started screaming fuck you at the audience.'"

Trudy felt like she *had* met Matty in the '90s though. He was a type. To a T. Bartending slacker, happily living off tips he never claimed and taking a class here and there. Seeing tons of shows because friends put him on the guest list. Smoking weed in the back alley. Sleeping with all the cute girls with black eyeliner and ripped tights.

She could just see him scowling at her from the audience as she leaned into a song, belted it into the microphone, the synthetic lace material of her baby doll dress cutting into her arms where it didn't fit right as she flailed on her guitar. The hot stage lights beating down on her, sweat trickling down her back. She stomped her feet in their oversized boots, swept her hair as Judy, their drummer, sizzled on the hi-hats. Becky fucking nailed her bass line, and for once, they hit the full stop just right, and there was Matty: middle center, never dancing, not even to their one good song. Toilet paper shoved in his ears, nodding, nodding like he knew everything.

***

Matty leaned back into the couch, his feet on the coffee table, his hands holding Trudy's feet, eyes closed. His breathing slowed as he edged toward sleep. The condo building radiated silence, except for one small noise above them that sounded like a marble dropping and rolling along a wooden floor. Then silence again.

A therapist once asked her where Trudy the Rocker had gone. Trudy just grinned and shrugged. "Trudy the Rocker fell apart. The band fell apart. I tucked her away somewhere. Got on with my life," she said. The therapist asked her if she could take a moment to look inside herself and find that old version of Trudy and check in. "Sure," Trudy said and sat very still and looked around inside her brain, and there was the old her, standing beside a deep dark chasm, just standing there, waiting.

"Waiting for what?" the therapist asked.

"She's either gonna jump or be forgiven," Trudy said. "Who knows."

***

Trudy thought maybe they would have sex in the morning, before work. Sex in the morning slowed the day down in a way that drunken midnight sex didn't. Trudy took a deep breath. She knew she had to work on her past self to work on this present self. She worried she would never understand anything, that her present self would just end up standing beside her past self as a third, whole new her looked in on them inside her brain. Both of them standing side by side at the chasm, not saying a word to each other.

The aquarium bubbled and the ice dispenser inside the freezer rumbled. Her phone softly dinged and pulsed on the kitchen counter.

She had quit therapy soon after that session, but some nights after she slid under the covers, she conducted an inventory of her day, listed all the things she had accomplished one by one. At the end of the inventory, she checked in on Rocker Trudy. It was easy to find her, just a shadowed speck, an outline of herself standing beside the chasm in dim blue evening light.

The therapist had suggested that maybe Trudy's former self could give it a rest, could try to sit down and relax. And Trudy agreed that would be nice. Sitting beside the chasm. The therapist suggested she could see if the other Trudy had anything to say. And Trudy said, "Maybe."

SQUAWK

Phoebe's third-grade class couldn't have recess last Friday because there was a shiny black bear lurking around. The children piled themselves around the classroom windows and watched him like a TV show.

The bear heaved its belly onto the black rubber swing seat and hung facing downward, its legs dragging behind it like anchors. The bear lumbered over to the slide and climbed up the wrong way. It pushed itself onto the merry-go-round, lay on its back, and stared at the clouds as they circled slowly above him.

The children craned their necks to see what the bear saw, but from inside it just wasn't the same. The children had mixed feelings about the bear playing on their equipment during recess. They wavered between pride and inconvenience.

"It isn't fair," whispered Heidi.

"I think he likes the swings the best!" shouted Drew.

Phoebe knew how she felt, but she had no words for those feelings yet, so she turned her back on the bear TV and stared at a patch of blank cinderblock wall. A small, quiet girl with a snuffly nose, glasses, and braids running down her back like train tracks, Phoebe chewed the ends of her crayons, had problems with long division and making friends. Today, because of the bear, she clenched her petite fists, raised her shoulders, and squawked like a bird. It felt good to squawk, and her voice reverberated off the chalkboard and through the tiny cracks in the seals of the closed windows. The bear's ears perked up as he continued to rotate slowly on the merry-go-round, metal warming his back. Then the bear's nose swiveled toward the window, filled faintly with the children's faces and reflecting the playground back to him.

The bear stood and sniffed his way over; a big bear face suddenly right next to the astonished student faces, separated only by a plane of glass. The children stepped back in one big herd. Jimmy barked like a dog—once, twice—and the big bear teetered onto its hind legs, thumped back down, and then walked away, moving his heavy hips into the line of suburban tract housing that surrounded the school, right past the house where Phoebe lived with her Aunt Susan, for now.

After the bear lumbered away math lessons started and no one, not even the teacher, told anyone what had happened, even though no one told them not to. Later, the teacher asked the students to draw the bear, and weeks later the bear became a kind of private mascot when the teacher had a small flag made depicting the best drawing. It flew on a tiny stand perched at the end of her big desk.

***

During recess the next Friday, the light turned crisp and bright, and the sky hit a certain miraculous shade of blue. Phoebe stopped hop-scotching and walked quickly away from the other children. A need so fierce arose in her so that she could barely contain herself. She planted her feet, and tilted her head up—mouth formed into a big round O, eyes squeezed shut, legs straight. Her braids swung over her shoulders like two big arrows pointing down. The squawk came from deep within.

As if responding to a signal planned in advance but never agreed to, the children circled around Phoebe, looked expectantly up into the sky, and thought about their bear, which already reminded them of all they couldn't put into words, now and for years to come.

PERSPECTIVE

No one's feet touched the ground. This was the first, most obvious, change to their daily lives. A kind of floating happened now: shoes, the soles of them, hovered above the sidewalk. People could still feel the rocks and rubble, but they were dull. No sharp pinches, no twisted ankles. A dumb change, many said. They always thought the future would be improved and exciting—flying cars and mind melding.

Hovering just above the ground did not seem groundbreaking, but it did allow for a slightly altered perspective. People stood a couple inches taller, able to see the world from just above where they'd once walked around making proclamations and assuring others that everything would stay the same.

They did begin to see things differently, and they realized maybe this is how real change happened: in ridiculous increments, by suspect means.

Susan picked some apples from the dying trees, their skins puckered and sour. Peter, hovering, clipped his toenails, one foot propped just above the edge of the step stool beside the trash can. Stark clipping, nails flying. These days, fingernails and toenails grew so rapidly. Why did this also have to be a new thing?

Truly, the changes weren't that impressive, evolutionarily. Each day, Peter rose from hovering above his bed, to rest his feet on the air just above the floor, to walk down the stairs he could feel but not touch, to put his hand on a solid cup of coffee, to be rooted to the cup as he hovered over his kitchen chair, as he glanced up to make sure that, yes, the sun had risen again.

LIGHT AND SHADOW

The early morning light untangled Kris from her bedsheets. She'd unplugged the alarm clock the night before to eliminate the bright red numbers that marked her days. Today was timeless. She'd decided in advance. The little dog curled at the end of the bed thumped its little tail when he heard her rustle. The sunlight clear and bright against her bedroom wall. Kris felt she could swim right through it down the stairs. She knew the oak tree outside her kitchen window waited with open arms, had already decided its leaves were perfect in both light and shadow.

MATH

What Dan wants is for everyone to enjoy some spring air. If he wedges the chair just right, the door won't slam shut from the breeze blowing through the open window, and his daughter's puppy will continue sleeping. The geometry of it kills Dan though, figuring out the best angle for the chair, figuring out this life and its indifference to logic. The chair should wedge in the door hinge, Dan should solve for *y* by finding a hypotenuse, and nice, quiet, fresh air should flow through his house with the puppy continuing to sleep.

But already Dan's reasoning is faulty because it isn't a puppy sleeping—it's a baby, a currently sleeping but more often crying baby. Once slick like a seal, it slipped out of his daughter following its own complicated computations, more impossible angles made right by a midwife.

Although he knows it's wrong, Dan imagines the birth like fitting the couch into the upstairs living room. No one thought it could make that sharp corner, except Dan's wife Roberta, all tape measure and confidence. Nodding her head and motioning "C'mon, c'mon" with her thin arms as Dan and his brother pushed.

And when it came, the couch entered all at once—past the little lip of the last riser and sliding through the doorframe into the living room, just like the baby spilled itself into the cold, bright, confusing night. Dan doesn't say any of this out loud as he sits at the kitchen table contemplating the chair and the door, but it's how he thinks about it, making the birth into hard-to-fit furniture and wishing the baby into a puppy so that his daughter's life might be less complicated than the one he imagines around the bend.

No one knows what will happen after a couch has rounded a corner. At first Dan hated that couch, too stiff, impossible to nap on, but then time passed and he came to love it, forgetting he had wished it bigger and fluffier and easier.

Dan will wedge the chair in the frame just right, making a triangle to keep the door from slamming. Air will flow, and he'll feel satisfied this small problem has a resolution. He'll consider finally getting that screen door. He'll come to love the baby that isn't a puppy nipping at toys and chasing its tail. He'll continue to follow after all the other complicated solutions, always a step behind, not working the problem exactly right but, eventually, discovering *y*.

WORK

The jazz music droned on and on. The same station streaming every day, like super sweet corn syrup. It made the employees tired, but no one asked for the music to be changed because it had embedded itself in their DNA. Everyone tapped softly in their cubicles. *Tippity tap-tap.* Slowing down and then speeding up again. Like a murmuration. Some people wore headsets and remained on hold with different music—sad, slow classical—sliding smoothly into their ear drums.

Continuing to work required endurance, continuing to tap when they all felt the tapping was irrelevant, what with global warming and overpopulation and diseases coming and going like traffic jams. But the tapping itself calmed them, except when Jim got mad at a client and typed with hard, heavy strokes.

Sue cleared her throat, and again. Sighed. Stood up and walked across the cubicle aisle to stand beside Jim, who said, "Oh, Sue, just fuck off." Sue thumped Jim's ear with her thumb and pointer finger. And he said, "Okay, okay. Everyone is so sensitive around here."

And the typing once again flowed into a sound river with a jazz background, and they continued to almost sleep until 5 p.m.

BERRIES

The bear gets hungry, as bears do. Berries, berries, berries. So many antioxidants. Sweat circles his snout as he dreams about some nice takeout from the vegan place on Fifth.

We're all famished these days, the bear thinks, *longing for all the stuff we can't have.*

Costco delivery. More pizza. It's a vicious cycle.

The bear continues to eat the berries, dries them in the sun, sneaks them into smoothies. He didn't ask for this escape, but he continues to take it. The sun shimmers on a hill. The trees bark their leaves open, yap, yapping in the breeze. The brambles prick and squeeze. The bear uses his machete sparingly, chopping out a way in. Soon, he's swallowed up and full.

PRECESSION

Reclining in the velvet armchair that he carted home from a thrift store last week, a glass of wine in hand, Michael asks why I'm dressed like a clown. He sometimes pretends to be rich and pretentious.

"It's the socks," he says. "Why?"

I look down at my outfit: striped socks with men's oxfords, flood jeans, and a boxy button-up men's shirt. "I don't know. I used to be worse," I say. I'm waiting in the doorway for him to stand up so we can go to the gallery crawl. Michael knows I'm waiting, so he remains seated. He crosses one leg over the other—fishes around for a cigarette, can't find one, sips the wine again. It's a red, a deep burgundy against the golden chair.

Michael's dark hair waves back from his face, his olive skin tanned from his landscaping gig. He likes to mix high and low in all aspects of his life. He has nice lips, a good build. Not my type but not-not my type. Michael always rests in the middle of my life.

I jangle my car keys between my fingers. Pull a single cigarette from my bag and hold it up.

Michael sighs, stands up, slips clogs onto his bare feet, and plucks the cigarette from my fingers as he steps out the door. He closes the door behind him as if I'm not there, as if I'm some kind of cigarette tree. I open the door to cool fall air—leaves scattered, the smell of crunchy decay. Michael takes a long drag from the cigarette, looks toward where the horizon would be if all these houses weren't in the way. He blows the smoke out in a long stream. "You have a great body. Why not show it off?" He drops the nearly unsmoked butt, stamps on it, and lopes toward my car parked at the curb.

"Think about the bonus package the lucky guy gets once he's initially only attracted to my intellect and searing wit," I say as Michael ducks into the passenger seat. I open and then slam my door.

"You've got a point, Kate." He laughs. "But could you take off those socks before we go into the opening? Trust me. I know people there and everyone always thinks we're dating."

I push in the cigarette lighter, push in the cassette, drive us downtown toward the sunset accompanied by Hank Williams—his twang, his guitar, his silky voice confessing sad, lost love. The streetlights pop on, and the dusk is apricot. The lighter pops and I press its rosy tip to my cigarette. I'm feeling good. My body hums under its disguise.

The gallery hops with its dressed-up patrons, cheese trays, and glasses of pre-poured pinot grigio, with its lighting and white walls covered with black-and-white photographs. Fractured bits of conversation bounce off everything. Hubbub. Humming. Murmuring.

I've put on lipstick, taken off the socks. Michael and I side hug just inside the entrance. A make-up hug. He sees some artist friends and leaves me to anchor myself near a photograph, a ceramic rabbit in shadowed profile, nails suspended from thin strings around its head. There's the edge of a window frame and the image looks like it was shot through some kind of gauze. I look at it for way too long, getting lost, as I can do. Michelle Gerard took the photo, the text panel tells me.

Michelle will eventually break Michael's heart. A year from now, she'll storm off, leave him standing, stranded, on the sidewalk of a small town, and I'll have to drive two hours to retrieve him. No hint of this now, of course. I don't even know Michelle Gerard until she walks over—all good-fitting silk and nice pants, all expensive haircut and bright smile. She sticks out a hand, strong handshake, good eye contact. "You must be Kate," she says. Bright smile again. Turquoise jewelry.

"I am," I say.

"My work," she says.

"Fabulous," I say, and Michael materializes at my elbow with a fresh glass of wine. It's a smooth joining up. That's how it begins. Michelle. Future firestorm. That night, just a cool artist.

The three of us leave together to get a bite, happy at this moment, fitting together like a puzzle as we smoosh into a booth, order drinks and small plates. Michelle has a pure magnetic energy. I almost want to kiss her, so I know Michael does. They make plans to meet up in the morning. Michael wants to take her to the donuts and ammo place the next town over. A tester date.

Michael and I drive back to his place—no Michelle, he's taking it slow. He plops back into his velvet chair, clicks on the cable to the opening scene of *Casablanca*.

"Well, we have to watch this," I say, scooching on the floor to use the chair front as a backrest between his legs. We both smoke, the people in the movie smoke, we're all in it now, feeling the same stakes as the characters. The bar, the piano, Bergman's luminous lips.

"Now, there are people who know how to dress," Michael says, pointing at the TV, pointing at my socks, back on my shoeless feet.

"Umhmmm," I say, not wanting to get into it again.

"Men are afraid of me," I say.

"They are," he says, his eyes on the screen. "It's true."

"Michelle," I say.

"Donuts and ammo," he says.

"You'll fuck," I say.

"I certainly hope so," he says. "Open that other bottle of red on the kitchen counter. I'm getting a second wind."

I push myself up and turn toward the kitchen, its countertop dimly aglow from the stovetop light.

"Here," he says, handing me his glass. I reach for it—our hands touch as I grab the stem, my big shirt showing some skin Michael can't see because his eyes are on the movie.

He glances at me and we kiss. Just like that. Out of nowhere. A long kiss that's electric and warm. We slide onto the couch, like school kids. Michael grinding into me, me grinding back. Body to body. So much tongue.

Snappy dialogue and cool cocktails blink from the TV into the night.

***

Morning, and we've fallen asleep tangled together on the couch. John Wayne now wanders along on horseback, stuck in his dusty life, in an endless horizon across the TV screen.

Michael opens his eyes. Doesn't move his head. "Wow, who started that?" he says.

"Not me," I say.

Michael sits up—his legs draped over my body. He's pantsless, only his boxers on. I'm fully clothed. "Had to be you," he says. "I had no intention of ever kissing you."

The morning sun seeps through the big front window. "Is that right?" I say.

I hear a muffled door slam somewhere, birds chattering. A car alarm down the street. John Wayne nods his head and lifts his big silly hat. And I see through the picture window Michelle walking down the street, looking at house numbers, gorgeous in the morning light. Her casual clothes so exacting in their casualness. Bright sneakers, dark blue jeans, snug-fitting tee with a heart at its center.

I tap Michael on the shoulder and he jumps into last night's pants and runs up the stairs looking for a new shirt. "We'll always have Paris," I yell up to him.

"What?" he says.

"The Germans wore gray. You wore blue," I mumble to myself.

I'm rumpled and glue-mouthed, picking up our glasses on my way to the kitchen, where I'll show myself out the back door. I have my socks in one hand, shoes in the other. Happy to leave my car parked out front and walk home. Happy to feel the breeze ruffling my hair after it tosses the tops of the trees lining the sidewalk, the solid walkway warm against the soles of my feet. Happy to slip through a world with a sky this crisp and blue. "I think this is the beginning of a beautiful friendship," I say to myself.

TWO BEARS

My brother has hit two bears in two different states with his piece-of-shit car. Each time, both bear and car have survived. It's a draw in his eyes: Bear 2, Eddie 2. Eddie is waiting for his next chance to really take a furry bastard down so he can make some jerky, get a rug done for the rec room.

I say maybe he should just get a hunting license and kill the bear like a normal redneck. Eddie takes a long swig of his tall boy, looks me dead in the eyes for way too long, then gazes at the fallow field beyond his property. "Now, why would I do that?" he says. "That has nothing to do with fate."

Eddie is a weird one. He's the sibling who stayed close to home, still works in the mechanic shop with Uncle Virg. Chews tobacco; wears a bandanna, camo pants, work boots. The whole deal. But he's into tarot—reads cards on the side while people wait for their cars. There's a rabbit's foot in his front right pocket right now. Bet you.

"Fate my ass," I say. "You're just a really lousy shot." Which is true. As a kid, I was the one destined for down-home success. I got my deer every year. I won the demolition derby at the county fair. Twice. I dated a girl named Darla Jean. For real. But it turns out I left, and he stayed. Now I'm back visiting and checking out the dent in his Ford from the recent Tennessee bear that loped into the woods afterward, never turning back. Like, *Car? Whatever.* Or that's how Eddie seemed to see it.

Eddie crosses his arms over his chest, feet in a wide stance with his back to me. "Can't figure out what I'm supposed to learn from this," he says. "Goddamn universe." He throws down his beer can and strides into our parents' farmhouse, which is now his farmhouse, minus the actual farm. "God. Damn," he says, not looking back.

I pick up the can, follow him into the cool, dark kitchen, where he's fixing himself a sandwich. I've spent so many years following Eddie, and I just step right back into it when I'm here. He makes a second sandwich, leaves it on the counter, like a little raft adrift. I scoop it up, follow him into the dining room, which is also the living room. My twelve-point deer head is still mounted on the far wall, hooves turned up below it for hat pegs, a Virg's Auto baseball cap tipped over the one on the right.

The cards are in a neat pile waiting at the center of the table, wrapped in a clean, red bandanna.

"What in the hell you doing up there anyway?" Eddie asks, face nuzzled into his bologna as I sit down. The cards are a bigger question between us. A big, quiet question.

"Working, living. You know, having a nice life," I say. "Like a pretty life—with a lake, something more than here. I have goals."

"Uh-huh," he says, wiping his hands carefully on a paper towel.

Eddie unwraps the deck. He taps it. "Shuffle them," he says. "Think about your question, then pick a card." I notice his hands, even clean, have taken on the grime of a lifelong laborer—grit permanently packed into the dry skin cracks, a soft line of dirt under his fingernails. They're strong. And steady. He passes me a paper towel. "Clean your hands first," he says. "Don't go messing up my cards."

Instead of wondering about my own questions, I wonder about Eddie, the car, the bears. The first was in Kentucky, on a road slick with rain. Eddie slid into the bear and pushed him over a guardrail, the car dinging against the metal like a big bell. That bear disappeared, Eddie says. *Poof.*

I think about the why of Eddie keeping score and his waiting for the universe to kill him. I let all these thoughts swish in my head. Back and forth in my brain, swishing like mouthwash, and then I pick a card. I flip it over and Eddie does a quick inhale.

"Whoa," he says, and the color fades from his face. He deflates right there on the spot.

"What?" I say. "It's just a card, Eddie."

"Give me some time," he says. Eddie studies his hands, then the card, then he stares out the window at the afternoon breeze hitting the tree tops. He looks anywhere but at me. Finally, he pushes his fingers down onto the table, leans toward me a bit, and says, "The Tower." He sits back in his seat. It looks like he's found his center again. "This is the *Oh Shit* card, Joey. People think The Devil or Death are bad? No. This is it. This is the *You're Fucked* card. Bad shit is going down, man. Wow." He leans back in his chair, raising the front legs off the floor, crossing his arms over his chest. "You need to be careful, dude. There's no going back. The Tower's on fire and it's just fucking singeing everyone in it. Do you see that?" He leans forward again, thumping down his chair legs, and taps the card with his thick pointer finger, once, twice. "You've either got to master it or be destroyed, man. We're talking serious trauma, Joey. What in the fuck."

I feel like I've unfairly manifested something, that I cheated by not having my own question and using Eddie's life instead of mine, just like I did when we were growing up. I just followed him around and didn't have to make my own decisions. I got into trouble because Eddie did. I dated Darla Jean because Eddie told me to. The first decision I ever made on my own was driving away from it all. Getting in my car and leaving the farm, Darla Jean, Mom, Dad, Eddie. And maybe the moment I turned the key in the ignition started all the steps that led to this card on the table in front of me. The bears, the farm, and the dart that seems to have stuck Eddie to this spot forever.

"Can I get a do-over?" I ask. "And maybe a beer?"

Eddie thumps into the kitchen. I hear the refrigerator door open and close. He comes back with two tall boys and a sponge to wipe the table. He wipes around the card—doesn't touch it again the whole time I'm there. The Tower just continues to burn for the next three days. "There are no do-overs," Eddie says. "You know that, Joey. You learned that a long time ago."

HARRY, SECURED

Harry didn't mean to run away from home. It was a compulsion, the gathering together of a few things—a baseball card, his father's wristwatch, a tiny blue marble—and then making a peanut butter sandwich and filling the thermos with orange juice. With everything in place, he left his mother, out into the yard to become something better, something he couldn't yet name.

The front door closed with a satisfying click behind his blue sneakers. His back still touched its wood, felt the pulse of his home rising and falling behind him. The apple tree in his front yard towered like a sentry. Climbing the four planks roughly nailed into the side, he pulled himself up among the branching arms. Harry felt his calves straining as his sneakers got some traction. He sensed his body growing stronger right there on the spot, spurred on by this new, decisive action. He wedged himself into the best crook in the tree and took stock. *Not my life anymore*, is what he thought. *Living here now.*

Below him, his stately house, the symmetrical brick, raggedy bushes, and near the driveway, his wagon and a ball he played with yesterday. He could see the lumpy shadow of his mother as she traveled from kitchen to living room. The tingle of deception ripped through the soles of his feet, rising up through his belly, heart, and head. "She doesn't know," he whispered. "I'm gone, and she doesn't even know."

Harry hugged the tree, its bark stiff and sharp against his skin, like whiskers. His father had died the year before. In this new life, he understood, he would have to navigate all by himself, forever. He would pull himself up from the soft muck, up into something like this hard tree.

He waited for a revelation, for a kind of calm to descend over him and prove he enjoyed this new rebellion. He hugged the tree. Listened to some quick-witted birds singing their songs like little staccato punches into the daylight. A squirrel scampered by in its diligent search for nuts. Then silence. Time passing, pushing in on him. The collapse of his intentions came like a shove to the gut. Done.

***

Harry sighed, shimmied himself down, walked the driveway, up the brick steps to the front door. He had to ring the bell because he'd locked himself out. His mother absently patted his cheek, looked for a long second at the thermos in his hand, and then continued on into her adult world. "Harry, you should wash your hands," she said. "Try to be a good boy."

Clean, cold water slid everywhere, endless from the tap, as Harry soaped his hands in the kitchen, white-and-yellow tiles, a black-topped table with metal legs and matching chairs. His life would be infinite. This was clear to him now.

His mother kept all the non-kitchen stuff in the drawer beside the silverware. A ball of twine, a flashlight, some stray candles, safety pins, crayons, spare batteries. Harry pushed his hand through the mess, pulled out a screwdriver with a stiff black and red handle.

He tightened every screw in the house, from the light switch plates to the Bakelite handle on the chrome toaster to the base of the stand-up lamp in the living room. Harry secured each one, twisting, twisting, twisting. The give of the blade inserted into the metal, the exacting turn of his wrist. The driving down tighter until he couldn't anymore. Until he had fastened himself in place. Until he became this new boy who never untightened, ever.

EVERYTHING OKAY

Back when Emily first wore a wedding band, the ring radiated energy—love, or the ritual of love, as demonstrated by a raucous riverboat wedding, a great watery celebration despite their worries about family and exes and friends. One day, after a few years, all that energy had worn off, the ring's symbolism dissipated into the air, the band a deadweight. So, even though she still loved Ralph, Emily slipped off the ring, nestled it in her sock drawer in a little box.

No one seemed to notice. This surprised her. Emily thought maybe she emanated the energy of a Married Woman, like an overly floral perfume, but then she remembered no one had flirted with her before she got married. Not that kind of a woman maybe, so why would it be any different now? Too sure, too smart, too direct with her eye contact for most men—except for Ralph, who just stepped right in like he'd always been there, without fanfare flirtation or grand gestures, just walking along beside her on Main Street as she ran some errands, stopping to pick up dinner rolls at the bakery and some feta from the Greek place down a side alley.

Ralph liked wearing his ring. Even with it snug on his finger, women came on to him with corny lines about how they'd been staring at his hands, how smooth they looked, how capable. He loved Emily and wanted people to know, he said. She agreed—he should wear the ring. Ralph clearly didn't understand the extent of his good looks.

Maybe a bit too handsome for Emily's tastes even. Through the years women sometimes felt the need to hate her so they could lust after Ralph without the burden of thinking about his wife with any empathy. But Emily didn't care. She didn't like being a wife—didn't like the label or the way her own personality melted into his, and how others chose to define her, and how sometimes mail came addressed to Mrs. Ralph Scotch, someone she didn't know.

She threw those envelopes into the trash without opening them, which got her into some trouble with relatives and a few credit card companies. But Emily wanted to make a point. She was still in charge of her own life, thank you.

Today, Emily walks along Main Street, running errands, running into some of the same people she's run into for the past fifteen years. Everything seems alight with meaning for her today. She loves where she lives, wants to hoard it for a little while. She wears a T-shirt in November, the sky bright blue and the fall leaves giddy with color, and everyone, including her, makes happy eye contact. This surprise good weather has put phones in back pockets, left computers at home with half-written emails, allowed people to remember what it's like to walk for walking's sake. Emily considers the T-shirt shop's window display, stopping her momentum to consider buying the one with the octopus on the front. She's already wearing the one with the smart-looking rabbit holding a beer. Emily doesn't feel like walking inside the shop's dark interior, so she puts a pin in it for another day, decides to head toward the river.

Emily spies Ralph up ahead of her. Walking along, smiling, looking at the world, even though he normally rushes everywhere. Ralph pushes toward his future, not stuck in nostalgia like Emily can sometimes be. She wants to get his attention, but he outpaces her, so far ahead she knows she can't catch him, and she hates to yell.

A woman—maybe someone she met at a party over at the Randolphs?—rushes out of a store and grabs Ralph's arm. He startles and then stops and hugs her. Emily stops in her tracks. Ralph and the woman smile at each other, smile lines curling. He likes her; she likes him. Friends. Emily knows that. Ralph isn't that kind of guy.

The friends now stride along, chatting. The woman does look familiar. Maybe from last week's concert at Union Hall? With the carefree way they move through the world, it's like Emily is watching herself meeting Ralph for the first time.

It isn't like that anymore with Ralph, she knows. Difficult and complicated, Emily fills him with competing, illogical emotions. She knows this. He knows this. Sometimes these days they find themselves walking down the sidewalk, side by side, not talking. Not fuming either. Just not speaking, because silence can be so much easier. But now Ralph talks, jabbers easily with this woman, hands rising and falling in animation.

Ralph and the woman turn the corner and Emily feels a zap of relief. Back to her lonely self and down this familiar street. The bookstore, the post office, the copy store, the diner. The thrift boutique, the corner store, the gas station. Each one like a metronome, counting out the seconds of her life. Her hands free and bare, no mittens or gloves in November, just her purchases thumping against her side in a canvas sack. Her world expanding in front of her. She wants to run into an old friend, someone she can tell it all to. But here, now, at the edge of town, it clears out. She's the only one on the sidewalk. She nudges her hands into her pockets, stops and squints up at a tiny bird singing from a sycamore tree.

A honk-honk on the road in front of her. Ralph waves. Emily lifts her hand on instinct. Later, he'll tell her how beautiful and happy she looked standing there with her head cocked, listening. He'll say the sun was shining in her hair in this way that made her look younger and reminded him of the day they met. He'll reach for her shoulder, touch it gently. "Everything okay?" he'll ask.

FREDDY

The lake has a mind of its own and I never catch it when it changes. The flat, glassy reflection I just photographed and sent to Freddy has already shifted into ripples disturbing the upside-down underworld I was just wishing I lived in.

It's sweater-with-sandals weather. Fall is coming. A few trees along the shoreline have turned defiantly red. The rest are holding off. This is my favorite time of year, no matter how crappy I feel.

"Nice." Freddy texts back. Sends a pic of the sandwich he made for lunch.

I plan to sequester myself from the world for a few weeks. Just closed up shop and jumped in the car. The lake house is shared between family. Freddy being the only family member I'm speaking to at the moment, he got the text. He knows I'm here. I've met my let-family-know obligation.

The house is musty and dark—I've set up a folding table and chairs on the dock, strung up my hammock nearby. I don't love the house. I love the water, and I need some time to think.

Someone's dog saunters over to say hi. Where he came from, I have no clue. He decides to adopt me on the spot. His collar reads SAM, so I call him Sammy. A big brown mutt of a dog. Sammy thumps his tail on the rotting wood every time I look at him.

"Sammy," I say. "We've got some shit to figure out." He lies down. "Good boy," I say.

***

I own a little flower shop called Leaves & Leafing. Plants with a book exchange on the side. I like being my own boss. I get by and I don't have greater ambitions, so I've surprised myself with my recent discontent. Maybe it has to do with disowning family (excepting Freddy) and disconnecting from friends and having to put down my cat Skinny Pants. Maybe it has to do with Greg dying. I'm alone and confused and feel like I need a good talking to.

I'm pretty sure I'm going to have to do this by myself until I hear truck tires on the gravel road: It's Freddy, who has apparently mistaken the photo for an invitation. Carting in a big bag of groceries, turning on every light in the house, and taking down my hammock and stuffing it back into its sack as he saunters toward the dock and me in my chair.

I'm sighing and waiting and hoping he'll leave soon because he's all I've got and I don't want to jettison him too.

"Josie, yo," he says. "Aunt Franny just made stuffed shells. They're in the fridge." He tosses the stuffed hammock back and forth like a baseball he's going to throw my way. "Haven't been down here in forever, so when I got your text, I was like, what the hell, and here I am." He lies down flat on his back on the dock, hands behind his head, always comfortable in his skin. He crosses his ankles.

"Sorry about Greg," he says.

"You didn't even know him," I say.

"But still. It's the thing to say, so I said it. The fact I didn't know him is on you."

That's true. I keep my love life separate from my family life, even as the latter has dwindled to just Freddy, who tells everyone everything.

"You might have liked him," I say, trying to be fair. "But it doesn't matter anymore."

Freddy kicks his boots off. "I'm gonna stay here until you feel better, Josie."

"You're gonna be here a long, long time then," I say. "I enjoy being alone now. I'm not like I used to be. That's the first thing to know. Oh, this is Sammy. Not my dog." Sam lifts his head on cue, then slips back into his dog half-sleep beside me.

Freddy closes his eyes. He uses my packed-up hammock as a pillow. Little waves slap against the dock. After a while both boys are snoring, and I decide without much forethought to steal Freddy's truck because I see no other way to fuck with him.

I roll away in neutral and then I'm out on the highway, windows down, Freddy's shitty country music playing through the speakers. I drive to the liquor store, then stock up on snacks at the gas station. I lean against the truck that isn't my truck, thinking about a life that isn't my life that maybe I could try and lead. I crack my neck, roll my shoulders. Lean some more.

It's getting dark and I figure Freddy is awake by now, after getting eaten by mosquitoes. He's in the cozy lake house, which is still lit up, the oven preheating for the shells. He's found a baseball game on the transistor radio and given Sammy water, a blanket, some dry cereal he's found in the back of the cupboard. Freddy will be certain I'm returning. He'll set the table for two. I snap open a mini bag of chips, eye the six-pack in the passenger's seat.

Freddy would have liked Greg. They would have fished together and smashed through the woods on their mountain bikes. No questions asked. I told Greg I didn't have a family. I told Greg I loved him. Greg left this world anguished, thinking I had no one, which isn't true.

Fumes from the gas pumps mix with the smell of the popcorn machine drifting out from the station. The dusty horizon works its way to black-blue.

I text Freddy a photo of his truck, backlit by fluorescents. "Taking it through the car wash then I'll be home," I write.

"Nice," Freddy texts back. "Dinner's waiting."

LIKE RAIN

Mark held his hand out flat like a stop sign. "Wait," he said. And like magic, she did.

Julie waited. Mark knew this meant she thought he had something to say, that he had a chance.

"What?" she said, stomping her foot like a pistol shot. This made the bookshelf in their entryway wobble. Julie's face blinked blank, flat and white as a paper plate.

"I just wanted to say I don't want you to leave like this. Why does it have to be so . . . trite?" Mark said. He lifted his arms into a shrug. He tried to look eager and charming, like he could be sometimes, hemming and hawing or hedging his bets, he could never get his clichés right. Mark wasn't good at improv, unlike Julie, who could grab the spatula someone handed her on stage and break into a meaningful song about cooking implements with accompanying dance steps. "I mean you're storming out of the house," he continued. "*Storming*. Not very mature. Did you think of the cat, the plants, me?" He did think better of putting himself at the center of that list. "Did you think of the cat, Julie?" Mark picked up their big fat tabby, Jimbo, who didn't look in Julie's direction, just stared at the jade plant in the opposite corner.

"Yes, I've thought about the cat, Mark. Fuck the cat," Julie said. And she took a step forward, grabbed the doorknob, and opened the door so fiercely the fern by the window trembled. "Everything in this house is unstable. Even the golden pothos is dying," she said, hiking her knapsack higher up on her back.

Mark put Jimbo down—back feet, front feet. The cat leaned into a walk toward his food bowl, his one true love.

"This house sucks, Mark," Julie said, watching Jimbo go. "It was a mistake. You were right all along." A waft of pot smoke floated in, one of the only signs of life for Timmy, their housemate. Julie never said words like *fuck* or *suck*. Generally, she found swearing untidy. Her language made Mark break into a sweat.

"We had an understanding," Mark said. "We said it was an open relationship. We agreed on that."

"In theory," Julie said. "We agreed in theory, Mark."

Mark considered that—the many theories they had agreed upon. Julie shifted slowly from side to side, a moving target. He thought about the house, the cat. All the plants he'd have to water living here alone. *Fuck the plants*, he thought.

***

The day they first saw the house, Mark had been skeptical about the whole idea of having a home, of ownership. He saw himself as a Renter with a capital R; he saw himself as Uncommitted with a capital U. "It seems a bit small, Julie," he said, "and pricey. We'd have to get a roommate to afford the mortgage. I mean . . ." He squinted up at the little house that did seem filled with a kind of optimism, with the sun slanting just so and the crooked sycamore tree in the small front yard. A tree that would soon strangle their sewer line with its roots, but how could they have known?

Julie mentioned coziness, romantic togetherness. She didn't mention the future, but she turned toward him in the afternoon light, and her black hair followed, glinting. She smiled and thrust her arms out at her sides with a kind of Mary Tyler Moore opening-credits flair. "My arms open this wide," she said. "That's all the space I need, Mark." They both knew this not to be true, but in that moment, it seemed possible. Her blue eyes did that electric lighting up thing. A great performance.

Mark didn't mention anything about his arms or how long they were. He worried about the roof and how much life was left in the furnace. But he hugged her that day, and in an uncharacteristic fit of abandon, he thrust his hands out parallel to the ground and spun madly around the front yard like an airplane. He banked and twirled until the front yard, the trees, and the house itself convulsed around him, and then he fell like rain.

"It's perfect," he said, breathing hard, lying, but also not lying.

***

This was how hindsight worked, he realized as he looked at a not-smiling Julie awash in afternoon sunlight, her two suitcases standing sentry. It seemed like she'd gotten so tall in the last year.

"You've grown," he said.

BOBBY THE BEAR

Bobby zipped up the suit. It fit snuggly around his belly and ended tucked up under his chin. The full-length mirror in the bathroom barely got all of him: a chubby bear with a Bobby head. The suit still smelled new and with his low-grade asthma had him breathing a little heavy. The bear head itself, much heavier than expected, clamped onto the body. The eye holes were a little tricky and didn't hit right at the sightline.

But, there now, a happy bear. Standing in his bathroom waving back at his bear self, turning to see his little bump of a tail, swiveling his paws this way and that. Bobby gave a little jump. The bottles on the dresser behind him wobbled.

Bobby worked as a home inspector. He'd thought he'd use his liberal arts degree differently, but at least the idea of "home" interested him. The stuff people left behind, the choices they made about décor and landscaping. *Each home is a portrait of its owner*, he thought on his good days. His curiosity, which had gotten him into trouble at different stages of his life, came in handy with this job, and he got to keep his own hours. He could set Friday aside for me-time. He could eat brunch every day of the week, which he didn't do, but telling himself he could made a big difference in his one-person-company morale.

He served as an admin for the local home inspectors' Facebook group, liking articles people posted about property sales in the region and asking people to keep it clean when they got out of hand with the jokes. Judy and a few of the other inspectors organized weekly in-person coffee meet-ups on the edge of downtown where they complained and gossiped about uptight real estate agents. Sometimes they all went to baseball games. Sometimes they walked in the park and identified birds. Home inspectors were a weird group—not what a person would expect from working people who crawled through attics and set radon tests.

***

Bobby had dreamed of the bear suit off and on for a year before taking action. One day he checked the site and, finally, there was a good sale. He double checked his measurements, confirmed the return policy by phone, and pressed the BUY button on his screen.

The box came on a Friday, his me-day, and so he had time to open the bear suit up, air it out, think through actually putting it on. *The why. The why.* Bobby set the suit up in a chair in his breakfast nook. He sipped his coffee and gave it a strong once over. Petted the thick synthetic "fur," which reminded him of the nubby wall-to-wall carpet people sometimes used to cover up bad flooring. The why of the bear suit flip-flopped inside of him. A longing. A strange, secret longing.

***

Sometimes, even though they weren't supposed to, homeowners stood around as Bobby poked through the house they'd lived in forever. They followed him, apologizing for the fireplace or the furnace or the shitty paint job in the hallway. They talked of regrets, what they'd meant to do to the house but couldn't afford, or how they'd run out of time or lost their job or their wife. "There's no judgment here," Bobby always said, trying to reassure them that the inspection was not a direct commentary on their worth as a person. He just looked at things in the house and informed potential owners what was in good shape and what was in bad shape, and tried to give context to what good and bad meant.

"It's all objective. Everything," he said. "Remember that. A crack in the sidewalk is just a crack in the sidewalk, wherever it shows up." The owners, rarely reassured, sometimes gave him snacks or even lunch, which Bobby wondered about as far as bribes and ethics went. Even so, his final reports often offended the owners and alarmed the buyers. "I'm just doing my job," he said to himself and to his fellow home inspectors, who nodded in agreement.

Bobby liked to think of his reports as a real chance to put his university degree to use. He'd taken enough creative writing classes to get a minor, and he'd written a few stories for the school newspaper, too. He liked to think of each report as an article with his byline. Some buyers—those with their own uniquely under- or over-used liberal arts degrees—complimented his writing skills. He learned to shrug and push his arm away like a working-class guy. He learned to pull on the brim of his cap.

***

Agitated after weeks spent posing in the mirror from every possible angle, Bobby took to walking his quiet neighborhood streets late at night in the suit. He nudged open the screen door to avoid its creak, held it until it closed to avoid the bang. Gingerly, he thumped down the porch stairs, creeping across his small yard out to the hard blacktop. He thanked the Lord for the dim streetlights along Elm Road. During these walks, he immediately felt a real kind of freedom, something he could get lost in if given the chance.

It didn't really explain the why of the bear suit, but when he detoured into the little patch of woods at the edge of his neighborhood and started skipping and swinging his arms like a bear in a kind of suburban animation movie, his heart broke free from all burdens and anxieties.

Heavy, awkward, and still provoking a tinge of asthma, the bear suit left him panting after most of these jaunts. He needed to get into better shape and hydrate more, but still, he felt the potential, especially after he practiced dancing along to the prize-winning Fursuit Competition videos he found on YouTube. He practiced in the early morning, and that cardio really increased his lung capacity.

***

Later in the summer, the housing boom caught all the home inspectors unawares. Their weekly in-person coffee klatch worked itself into a low simmer. Home inspectors burned out left and right, deals fell through, prices rose, and buyers became litigious. Nothing sleepy about it anymore. Where they once talked about weekend escapes and the new kayak they planned to buy, the inspectors now commiserated about pissed-off owners, agents, and buyers from out of town who asked them where they could get a deal on a new washer. "Not in my job description!" Bobby almost-yelled at his colleagues.

"Why are they doing this to us?" Judy asked, quietly sipping her Frappuccino.

I'm a bear, I'm a bear, I'm a bear, Bobby thought to himself, tapping the table in time with his paper cup. He fished the last of his cappuccino's foam out with his finger. He needed to keep centered. It rang through his body, this internal mantra, and it helped him distance himself from his fellow inspectors. It also distanced himself from, well, himself, he guessed.

***

Naturally, Bobby started wearing the bear suit to inspections. Or, to be more exact, carrying the bear suit with him in his hockey gear bag and putting it on during an inspection once he'd checked the house out to make sure nobody was around. Risky behavior, especially in mid-September, with Bobby overworked and slightly frazzled.

A Wednesday 1:45 p.m. inspection popped up when he checked his calendar after his morning aerobics. He called the owner, Chuck Hamilton, as he drove over to the North Hills. Chuck confirmed the appointment, confirmed no one was home. In fact, he and his wife Meg were on the road themselves, driving into Philly, looking for a good place for lunch. Did Bobby have any suggestions? Bobby extended the phone away from his face to look at it incredulously. "No," he said. "I don't do restaurant recs. I'm a home inspector."

"Okay, then," Chuck said. "Have at it." Before they hung up, he reminded Bobby that they'd fixed the roof last year. "Gotcha," Bobby said. "I'll give it a gander."

The Hamiltons' home was up a little rise in the neighborhood and had a nice view out to some woods, fall leaves just starting to show. After he walked around the exterior, Bobby grabbed his tool belt, phone, water bottle, and his hockey bag.

At 2 p.m., the sun streamed through the foyer. The house looked nearly empty, a kind of just-threw-everything-in-boxes-for-the-movers vibe, clearly nearly moved out to another home that some other inspector had inspected, which had its own set of unique objective problems not connected to this house. *No one home*, Bobby thought, and he felt it too, a kind of empty space in both the home and in his heart. Bobby put on the suit.

Bobby's bear steps echoed through the living room and spotless kitchen. He secured his bear head and bopped up the stairs, two at a time. Now that he was in shape, the bear suit made everything easier for him, even though wearing the suit made the actual inspection strenuous. He walked with long strides down the hallway, his tool belt gently clanking against his furry thighs, checking the venting in the bathroom, the fan. He ran the faucet, flushed the toilet. Admired his round, beautiful bear head in the mirror above the sink.

He opened the door to the primary bedroom. It creaked on its hinges. There the mattress lay, mid-room, exposed like a big slice of white bread, bedding wadded in the corner. *Potential*, he thought to himself for no reason. *Still life*, he thought. The bear suit let him take a step back and see beauty in unlikely scenarios. He slid the dimming light switch, noted yellow staining on the ceiling, knowing he'd have to check out the source of that present or past leak when he climbed into the attic, whether they'd replaced the roof or not. Decent carpet. He'd revise it to "reasonable" later on in the report. *The carpet in the second-floor primary suite is reasonable for the age of the home.*

By the time he opened the next door, he'd fully entered his groove as both home inspector and bear. He glowed with forward action, ready to wrap up, de-bear, and drive home. Bobby used his phone's memo feature to record his assessments because the bear paws made taking notes impossible. He clicked the memo on. "Second-floor bedroom," he said, as he pushed the door open, stopped short of sliding on the light switch. A musty smell hit him. And there—dead to the world—snored a teenage boy, mouth agape, sheets askew. Maybe the Hamilton's son had a part-time job that had called him off, or maybe Mr. Hamilton was so concerned with finding a good sandwich he forgot about his son, sleeping in his room? Who knew. The kid's stringy hair and skinny naked torso seemed surreal in the tangle of sheets.

The walls were a dark green, and with the shades drawn, made the whole space feel moldy and earthen. The nearly reasonable carpet, tan. Clothes strewn everywhere, a small textile explosion. Nachos with congealed orange cheese rested on the dresser top along with a line of dusty sports trophies, a crunched beer can.

At first Bobby wanted to run away. A bolt of shame zapped up his spine. He was outfitted in a bear suit! How would he ever explain this to anyone? But then his eyes adjusted, and he saw the taxidermied animals and fish that lined the walls. They added to the chaos and confusion of the moment and inspired much introspection later on. Bobby could only assume the boy had killed these once-alive creatures. A twelve-point buck, neck curved just slightly to the left, hefted its impressive rack, a snapper tried to writhe free from its varnished oak plaque, and a pretty pheasant gawked at Bobby from the nightstand, a lampshade, dim bulb still burning, stretched up from its back.

Bobby felt a primal urge, no other way to describe it. The deer blinked and winked his way. He locked in with it. Deep in his soul, he felt a hunger that needed satisfying. Bobby slipped across the room, dodging clothing and a baseball mitt. Just as he lifted the buck's head from its nail, the sleeping boy opened his eyes.

After quickly unhanding the deer back to its wall, Bobby went electric and stood at attention. He tipped a pawed foot forward, toward the boy, his daily dance video training kicking in without a glitch. He waved at the young Hamilton like a creature from Disneyland, or, perhaps more accurately, from a lesser amusement park. Jazz hands. Jazz hands. Small kick. The boy, groggy as all get out and possibly still half-drunk, waved back, turned under his covers, and fell asleep again just like that. Bobby stood at attention again, counted to twenty, lifted the deer, cradled it in his arms, and carried it down the stairs to his car.

WOODPECKERS PECK TO ESTABLISH TERRITORY IN THE SPRING

The tree branches that run along Martha's path twist and loop like licorice whips, as she circumnavigates through a patch of wild garlic mustard and knotweed. A woodpecker drums a little *tat-tat-tat, tat-tat-tat*. Mid-March and the forest, dormant and muddy, has lost a tree here and there, giant roots upended from so much rain. A small trunk blocks her way. Martha grabs at the bark, swings her legs, one at a time, over to the other side. The whole valley sighs, subdued and still. Except the woodpecker. His exuberance unbearable.

Martha hasn't been on this trail for years. As she walks, it transports her back to a time when she wandered in these woods and her mother cooked her meals—gravies and roasts and soggy green beans—and Martha pushed the side door open after playing outside all day. What she remembers is her mother's back, curved toward a pot of steam, a wooden spoon, early evening light tipping through the window, a polka crackling from the under-the-cabinet radio.

Today Martha has some loose change in her front pocket, a cell phone in her back pocket, and a sinking feeling, even though these woods make her feel weightless, a little lightheaded.

Tat-tat-tat.

Her mother sometimes sent her out into the yard, to the edge of these woods to throw scraps onto the compost pile, which Martha could never seem to locate exactly, even though she asked again and again. She flung the soggy onion skins and potato peelings and fled back to the glowing house on the rise. She would soon have real things to fear, but back then, just the edge of this space was enough—the woods and the dark rippling shadows within and the sharp air settling down into the grass.

There had been a shack too, an abandoned shed on the edge of the property, wedged into a little slope so that the roof on one side stood nearly level to the yard. The rough shingles, black like razor stubble. The single window, blank and cracked like an egg. The structure remained unused and then it was gone. Torn down by her father, she supposes. Her memory of him: sturdy shoes, thick arms, and the smell of cigar smoke rising.

Skip to the day she played with friends at a neighbor's house. The Kodachrome sun lit the neighborhood. Children scampered, playing Bloody Murder across backyards. They looped in circles with braids and cut-offs and tank tops with spaghetti straps, knobby knees.

Birds chirping, the world continuing on. *Tat-tat-tat.*

She remembers her skinny legs, little clogs dangling from her feet. Then empty white space. The rest of the story. A big blank marshmallow of an idea. A cloud, a word bubble. Suspended. Floating in hot chocolate, which waited for her back at the house.

Martha continues through the brown woods. The sunlight muted. Her phone on mute, silencing the calls asking about the house for sale by owner. A flash of feathers and branches lift as the bird takes flight. Her solid steps onto the soft lawn leave an outline of where she's come from.

INTO THE NIGHT

The bear, brushed and groomed, sprayed lightly with sandalwood essence, shoulders back, head high, nudged the front door of The Fig with his paws right at 4 p.m.

He'd been bartending at The Fig for six months. The social nature of the gig suited him. Like not-working, but with a to-do list. Particularly, he enjoyed plunging the dirty glasses into three tubs to get them clean. He liked setting them neatly in formation like bowling pins on the rubber drying mat. He chatted while he worked. Fluid, easy.

The bear liked knowing people, but honestly, he didn't like people knowing him. The more regular his shifts, the more they knew and that just wasn't okay. Ted the actuary, for example—tan fedora, carefully folded white handkerchief in his front shirt pocket—had taken to calling him *bear*tender, and it took everything in the bear's being to not slash Ted's chest to shreds. Over the past few months, Ted had leaned on the bar, head in hand, elbow on the bar top, and asked questions about the bear's family, his birthplace, and hobbies.

So the bear started calling Ted Teddy, then Teddy Bear, and then My Little Teddy Bear, which Ted, in turn, did not appreciate. "C'mon dude," Ted said, dabbing at his forehead with the handkerchief. "Stop acting like you're coming on to me. It's creeping me out. You're a bear." And the bear shrugged, held up his paws in a mea culpa, and turned to make Judy an old-fashioned or Deesha a gimlet. The bear made a mean gimlet.

The bartenders had a cheater book behind the bar. They could look up drinks they didn't know how to make, but the bear just made drinks up once he heard the name. Who's going to second-guess a bear at happy hour? And this is how he came to be known for unknowable drinks. Concoctions he threw together so fast in the shaker that his own brain didn't have time to register the ingredients and he could never replicate them.

Each night at the end of his shift, the bear asked one of the other bartenders to make him a perfect Manhattan on the rocks. He liked hunching over the glass tumbler, stirring the big, fancy ice cube around in circles with a claw. Lingering, listening in on conversations. Learning secrets, guessing motivations. He stuck around until the place had cleared, then he swept up and tipped the stools onto the bar top. Sometimes he lit up a cigarette, pushed the illicit smoke out into the pristine air, let it float around, pretended it was the 1940s, when bears had room to roam. Time to sleep off entire winters.

Two a.m. and the bear pointed the remote, flipped through channels, clicked the screen blank. The bar dark and moody. Everything turned off so no one got any ideas about trying to come in. The bear watched the sidewalk instead. The big picture window framed the dark, rainy town. A skinny woman walked a little dog in a yellow raincoat. A sporty guy pumped a slick black bicycle. And then Teddy stumbled by. The wide sidewalk slid along the front of the building under his feet. Teddy, oblivious to the beartender, as he leaned against a lamppost, looking nothing like a teddy bear, the bear realized. Stretched, a little gray at the gills. Not cuddly. The bear wondered who had overserved him tonight. Teddy hugged the lamppost and looked out at the town while the bear looked at his profile.

We get these names we don't like, the bear thought, *and then we become those names*. No going back until a bear pulls up his stakes and makes a new life, taking on other definitions elsewhere.

The bear didn't mind roaming around from place to place—sleeping in ditches or a cave until he found a better home and settled in again. Teddy would stay stuck here though, that was clear. And the bear felt a little bad that he'd heard other people calling him Teddy Bear—that the bear himself had changed the structure of this place. He had no intention of staying for the repercussions.

He slid his big brown butt off the corner stool, tipped it upside down, and clambered back behind the bar to wash his glass, spray some air freshener, hide his ashtray. Silence like the deep woods, and the bear felt a longing, a true missing of all he'd left behind.

Teddy tilted himself toward the crosswalk, made his way across Fifth and into a shadow, eaten up by the night.

TRENCH COAT

After hours, Natalie's high school glows otherworldly. The memory of it will remind her of an art museum at night—the glass and polished floors, the distinct silence after a bustling day. But tonight she has not yet been to an art museum.

She has seen Boy George dance with wide open arms on MTV. She knows Duran Duran and Flock of Seagulls. She wears a black trench coat she bought at a thrift store. It hits her calves; slightly too big. It fans out, with a wide 1970s collar and big black buttons. Her favorite piece of clothing. Natalie can't know that in a week her mother will hide the coat and that she won't find it again until she's in her forties and going through a closet looking for her mother's mink stole. The trench coat, shoved to the back, will be too small for Natalie by then. When she last wore it, she hadn't finished growing. She'll clench her hands into fists, still standing in the closet, and refuse to cry as she dips her hands into its pockets. Her elderly mother will call up the stairs to ask what's keeping her so long. Natalie will pull herself together, of course. Of course.

But this night isn't the future; it's now. She's wearing the coat, and the high school has shut down for the day. The art club students plan to paint a mural in the gymnasium. Natalie isn't an artist and will never be an artist. She'll be an art historian. But this night she's here to support her friend Christie and to feel, she doesn't know, a kind of freedom. Just leaving her home and clicking her seatbelt and driving to the school, making that decision. Natalie feels amazing.

She wears sneakers with the trench coat. In a couple years, at college, far away from home, she'll wear faded red Chuck Taylors she finds at a thrift store, a little too small for her feet. But for now, she has on Adidas sneakers she bought at the mall with her mom. Natalie feels set free. The musicians on MTV seem radical, a voice for her generation. New Wave. She's cut her hair short on top and left a long tail running down her back. The front curls around her face. She wears pink lipstick, just a little, and some eye liner. Her skin shines like moonlight. Christie said she'd meet her by the water fountain near the auditorium, and then they could walk to the gym together.

Christie has to tackle a long list of chores before she can leave the house. The single-spaced typed list hangs on a wall right outside the kitchen. The list looks endless. It spills into two columns. Christie could never finish all the chores on it, ever. Yes, Christie said, that's her parents' point. She could always find something to do. Something more. And then she said, "Who types a chore list?" And they both laughed because no one types lists except Christie's mom, who types everything, even shopping lists, on her humming electric typewriter. It sits centered on a desk near the kitchen with a plastic cover over it. Natalie has never seen her in the act of typing, but evidence in the form of lists lies everywhere in their house. Christie just shrugged. "I hear the motor hum and her tapping at the keys sometimes really late at night. My mom says it's soothing. I don't know," she said. "I think she just wanted to be a secretary instead of a mom." And they both nodded at that because Christie's mom does not seem to love her children. Not the way Natalie's mom loves her and all her friends. Always wanting them underfoot, even as obnoxious teenagers. Natalie's mom takes her job as mom seriously, and at this moment, Natalie thinks she has a nearly perfect mom. She doesn't yet understand the ways in which she doesn't know how to think for herself.

When Natalie thinks back on this night, it feels pure and easy and without complication. She pulls open the thick glass doors and walks into the brightly lit foyer. She knows the freshman, even the sophomores, think she's cool. Natalie tucks her car keys into her coat pocket. Cool. She just likes being observed, in her trench coat, car keys in her pocket, feeling absolutely comfortable in this second-home building. What with track practice and volleyball practice, dances and school itself, she's there all the time and never gets lost in the hallways the way she used to just a few years ago.

Natalie leans against the wall next to the auditorium water fountain, taps her head back against it, one knee bent so her sneaker hits the wall too. The future remains unknown. Her hands in the pockets of her trench coat, fingering her car keys, waiting for her friend.

Someday she'll rewrite so much of this time of her life, but not this particular evening, because Christie arrives, not even very late, wearing her favorite Bruce Springsteen T-shirt under her brother's flannel shirt. She's happy because her mom let her skip drying the dishes for once. She rushes in, grabs Natalie's hand, and they run through the hallways to the gym, sneakers squeaking, hair lifting from their open faces.

CAUTION

Jill shoved her thick hair behind her ears and then raked it back toward her face. She rubbed the end of her nose, smoothed her hand across her cheek where freckles had started to scatter from working out in the early summer sun: June, with all the windows open and a tiny breeze pushing at the lace curtain in the living room. Her T-shirt sagged on her broad shoulders, her jeans shorts a size too big, the way she liked them. Early morning New England. She could hear the buoys clang in the blue water distance. The fog about to lift. The quiet house exhaled.

The glasses from the night before stood watch. She set them in the sink, tidied the chairs, and brushed some crumbs into her palm from the counter. Then she stopped stock-still, looking out the kitchen window above the sink, frozen for a moment. She let her focus blur to soft green and blue. She straightened her back, nudged her shoulder blades into formation. Took a big breath, let it out through her thin lips.

"Ready for coffee?" she yelled up the staircase, not too loud, but she wanted to be heard. The morning sun broke through the fog and scattered rays through the gauzy kitchen curtains. The membrane between outside and inside stretched thin. The cat sauntered across the wood floor and through the doorway into the living room to perch in the big window with the view of the maple tree, her tail slashing the air. Soon she'd twitch in big dreams of the hunt and kill.

Jason neared the top of the steps, paused. Jill could almost hear him up there breathing, looking down. He creaked the floorboards. Creaked them again. "Great," he said, down the staircase, trying for enthusiasm. She heard him retreat down the hallway toward the bathroom.

Jill stood in the center of the kitchen—oak floor, blue cabinets—holding the moka pot with both hands, its steel solid and industrial. Soon she'd set it on the stove and the heat would sputtle coffee from its spout and a new day would begin. A few birds hopped and sang at a distant feeder. "Okay, great," she said toward the staircase with an equally forced bounce to her voice. She knew he wouldn't hear her. Jill made the coffee, poured it into a mug for herself, for Jason. Thick, syrupy espresso that smelled like turned soil, which she followed with warmed milk.

This had been their routine now for ten years. Coffee together was a thing they did well. They did mornings well, almost always. Jill set a saucer on top of Jason's mug to keep it warm.

The night before had been a bad one. Jill understood now, had only recently come to understand and maybe sometimes sense, the invisible land mines embedded inside Jason's world, waiting to blow up.

She swung open the screen door, let it almost slap closed behind her, catching it at the last second with her heel. Her soles hit the painted porch floorboards with their own quick slap. She held her warm mug to her lips with both hands. That first sip of coffee. It changed everything for her, every morning. It couldn't be replicated. Jill tried to own the moment, whatever came next, whatever had happened last night.

She always felt—afterward—that the explosion could have been prevented. That she could have dismantled the mine before it left her blinking back tears in the middle of rubble. Maybe she could have thrown herself on top of it, defused it. But Jill knew what came next only as it was happening, often only after it was happening, not before. Always too late to stop it. A memory-jumble of regrets and should-haves and aha moments. Never at the right time. Until it was over. And that was no help whatsoever.

***

At the restaurant the night before, a place they both loved near the docks, had loved for a long time, the noise surged as they walked in—louder than usual, an insulated echoing that replicated the sea nearby—tidal waves of chatter and laughter mixed with the evening's heat. Jill noted the vibe, checked a little box in the back of her head, but walked forward toward the sweet and sour cocktail smells, toward the smoky anticipation of dinner. They sat at the edge of the dark bar. Candles flickered. Heated wax. Low slung but insistent music beneath it all. A magnetic hum. But things were already wrong.

***

Earlier, on their way to the restaurant, they had walked a trail through the little city park. It was beautiful out, dusk and the town's lights coming on, and the bay water shined and rippled in the dwindling early evening sun. Jill wanted to take a photo, had been thinking about the best composition and framing, so she missed the beginning of Jason's story.

Jason's pace slowed. He was saying something about his brother. Jill half-listened while she took out her phone and tried to get a good angle on the rippling light as it tilted itself into dusk with the town's church steeple in the background. His brother Rob had died by suicide years before. She knew that in the final months of his life he had filled plastic water bottles with vodka and walked around drinking all day. "Trying to get it over with," Jason had said. The police said there was no doubt about the suicide after Rob was found in his bathtub, that he'd made sure he got the job done. But that was years ago, before she knew Jason, back when he was still part of a family that he didn't speak to now. He wouldn't open their cards or letters, answer their phone calls, texts, or emails. "I have you," he said to Jill, "not them."

"But I never think about Rob anymore. I'm so far beyond all that," he said now, looking up into the leaves fluttering in the twilight above them. He buried his hands into the back pockets of his jeans. Did a little stretch of his back. Jason looked Jill in the eyes and smiled his sweet, tired smile. He took her hand and she swung their arms a few times, gave him a quick side hug, rested her head on his shoulder, and then pulled away.

Jill planned to post the photo later with a note about what a great night they'd had, already figuring she knew the math of their future. Then they entered the restaurant, and the noise, coupled with the dim light, should have given her a heads up. Should have sent a red alert, but didn't. And then suddenly (but, she would see clearly the next morning, not suddenly, because the whole day had been building to this moment), Jason said: "Johnny is fucking a twenty-year-old."

Not really talking like himself—Jason had his head tucked down a bit into his shoulders, and he looked through Jill, not at her. He wouldn't normally say *fucking* with such an edge to it. Jason usually stopped at *Can you fucking believe it?* He was that kind of guy, normally a bright optimist. But his brown eyes pinpricked to a faraway point now. This new fact shocked Jill nonetheless, since their friend Johnny was over sixty years old.

"That's gross," she said, casually dipping some bread into a mix of olive oil and balsamic. Eating it, relishing the mix of textures, the sweet oil with the acidic vinegar, the crisp give of the bread's crust. Frankie the bartender rattled his shaker and the ambient noise pulsed. Jill talked without thinking because she wanted to enjoy the bread and build a bridge to a more interesting, and less complicated, conversation where they might laugh and make jokes and have a nice date night out, because really, in the grand scheme of things, Jill didn't care who Johnny fucked. Johnny and the twenty-something could deal with their own lives, and she and Jason could gossip about it. That was that.

But Jason, who under any other circumstances on any normal day would just have agreed with her and moved on to other things, said, "I don't know. He's a good guy. I'm a good guy, too. What's wrong with Johnny dating a younger woman? Who cares?" In retrospect, Jill believed that she had to have known. But really, she didn't—not yet. Not right then. Not with enough time to stop. Circle the moment with a big red marker. Stop everything. Get the check. Go home. Stop. Talking. "If I had a twenty-year-old daughter, maybe I'd be happy Johnny was fucking her," Jason said.

Jason clutched his sweating glass of whiskey. He did not dunk bread. He would soon order another drink, a double. What had he said about his brother Rob when they were walking by the river? Jill should have paid more attention. Something reminded him of Rob? Someone from his family tried to text again . . . she didn't know. Jason, now almost a stone, sat across from her, and she knew if he did have a daughter he would most definitely care if Johnny fucked her. Right now, though, he sat in their nicely lit local place with the glass doors and the local art on the walls, but he also existed in his childhood, in the grip of some monsters and what they had done to him, to Rob. She didn't know. She couldn't ask. Only he could see this other world while they sat there waiting for the gnocchi to arrive.

And inside Jill something else lurked that transformed her and prevented her from stopping the escalation, the spiraling, kept her going further into the conversation of why Johnny shouldn't date a twenty-year-old, that Johnny had issues from high school he had never gotten over, wanting to date the prom queen and instead never having a real date until he turned thirty, never getting laid or not enough. "Johnny has issues, he's had them since he was a freshman, and I think if he just dealt with them, he'd be a happier person," she said.

"I don't give a shit about Johnny's high school issues," Jason said. He said that Jill needed to lighten up. She needed to stop judging everyone. What was she talking about? Johnny could help this young woman, who could instead be dating an asshole her own age.

"Help?" Jill said. "Johnny's going to *help* her?" She sucked in a little breath. She felt a little panicked. She smiled at Frankie, who gave her a little wave from down the bar as he grabbed and poured from another bottle to top off a shaker. Then his rat-tat-tatting before he poured again.

The night curved into a vortex from there—deep, dark accusations repeated quietly below the din of the festive crowd. Jason simmering with rage, and Jill not knowing how they'd gotten here but knowing what came next. Rob, was it Rob? His brother. Couldn't they just move on from Johnny and his fucking? The waitstaff at the bar, who knew them well, everyone knew their names, for instance, sensed something had fundamentally changed in the molecular make-up of their relationship this night. Jill supposed they thought she and Jason were arguing about money or family. An affair. Something close to a normal argument. A longtime marital spat. Frankie delivered the bill promptly without the usual chitchat after he'd cleared the plates, didn't ask about dessert. Everyone gave them a wide berth, all professionalism and head nodding. She thanked god for that.

***

Jill walked silently ahead of Jason on their way home, past the little shops that made up their town. Deep in her head, she only thought about putting one foot in front of the other, moving forward. She needed to process this situation, again, now numb to the world as it slid by. "I just wanted to have a nice night out," she said quietly.

"Yeah, right," Jason said.

Walking, walking, walking toward the streetlights, toward the intersection where she would turn left up the alley. Jason behind her. She felt him needing her and hating her, too—deep, in over his head, again.

She said over her shoulder, as she continued to walk away, "Come back to me."

And Jason muttered, "I'm trying. Believe me."

***

And then the rest of the complicated night unfolded, with more drinking and door slamming and stomping on the stairs. Jason sitting at the kitchen table yelling, pounding his fists once, hard, a slam that sent the cat up the stairs. "I can't do this anymore," he screamed.

"People are going to hear you," Jill hissed, a knee-jerk reaction that came right on his outburst's heels. Jason stoic at the table, neutral zero, not there anymore, not there, as Jill closed the windows to the cool night air before walking upstairs to sit in her chair in the far corner of the den. She tried not to say anything, but said things nonetheless, couldn't stop wondering how this started with Johnny fucking a twenty-year-old, knowing it wasn't about that at all, and later, Jason's heavy steps up the staircase from the kitchen and again up to the bedroom.

She knew he would fall into bed head-first, out cold, no usual fidgety night's sleep for him. Silence descended like a curtain, end of show. She took her own slow steps toward the bedroom.

***

Jill had fallen asleep beside Jason, thinking about what she would take with her when she left him, what she would leave behind, and how the cat would hate the small apartment she would rent farther from the water, but now the simple morning sun rose up bright and perky and she made coffee and poured a cup for Jason as he paced upstairs.

Jason would come downstairs in the next few minutes and, Jill knew with 100 percent certainty, apologize for the night before and call it a setback and talk about how as he got better the setbacks were shorter but roared louder. And Jill would hug him and rub his back without really understanding what had happened, but also knowing—entirely.

She'd think if they could just never leave their home again everything would be okay. If she just cooked for him and unplugged everything, if they lived in complete silence, it would be fine. They would be happy forever.

Jason's foot tapped the top step that always creaked just so when he came downstairs slowly. Jill sucked in a quick breath, knowing that a typical happily ever after would never happen, that they would be unhappy again in the future. Again and again. But they'd be happy today, and that calm would feel wonderful enough. In ten minutes, they would be happy again. Jill emptied her coffee dregs over the porch railing, turned toward the screen door, and made her way inside.

HONESTY

The steam rises, a choir rubbing up my round belly then swirling to a hallelujah at the ceiling. Thirty-six weeks, and I'm an island of flesh in this clawfoot tub. The water laps at me each time I shift, topsy-turvy, then settles flat, somber again.

The storm outside thunders down in heaving splats, polka-dotting the concrete, seeping into the house somewhere, I'm sure. Water, water, water. Heat and musk and love. That's what put me here in the first place.

I'd wanted a kitten, alone in the big old house, as it creaked and talked back. My green chair plump and prim. I wanted a kitten and I got a baby. That's the truth. It's hard to remember the timeline when you're kept in like this, when the rain never stops, when you're sure you've loved your daughter forever, even if she hasn't been born yet.

The water ripples. The room smells of frankincense. The rain will not relent. A cat cries in the night, soft and soggy. A slinky wail, then the tick-thump of the cat door as it steps inside like a spring breeze, some rustling leaves. The shake of water from fur. The rattle of bell on collar.

I hold my breath. Sink down farther into the water. The cat jumps to stalk the tub's rim—its tail a flag of surrender, its belly hanging low. Around and around it goes.

The baby settles inside me. Out there the world vanishes for a second, everyone penned in by a big fat circle and then it all releases again. Thunder, lightning.

The truth: The water will not stay hot.

The truth: I wanted a kitten, but my mother, she always said no.

THE VISITOR

The radio babbles a talk show in fits and starts. The emcee clears her throat and apologizes. The visitor wonders whether the radio plays all the time or if her host turns it off at night. The visitor turns the radio off. The ceramic fruit bowl sits in a dim shadow on the counter. Bananas, a couple of oranges, an acorn squash, and some onions. It's fall. A pan of just-finished granola, still warm, rests on the wooden countertop. The visitor pulled that together before she lost steam. A wooden island in the middle of the kitchen is covered: half a bag of potatoes, candles in holders, more candles, empty spice jars, a water glass, Post-its. The host swears he uncluttered the tabletop yesterday.

Clutter also smothers the kitchen table. A computer, more water glasses, a few colorful cloth napkins, a tennis ball, more candles, a small dish of salt, some folders, a pen (uncapped). Red chairs ring the kitchen table, vintage, from the 1950s, cracked vinyl and wood. Warm and homey. There's a tray with a decanter filled to the brim with whiskey, its two glasses hunkered in the corner.

An aloe plant on the windowsill, and outside the window, a bright sunny day beats down. The leaves, mostly off the trees and strewn across the road, used to be yellow and vibrant. The blue sky and the giant pine tree loom over everything. A skyscraper of a tree. The empty one-way street stretches like a Band-Aid. Yesterday, for a half hour, cars whipped by, driving the wrong way. This made the visitor sitting near the window nervous. She waited to hear a crash that didn't come.

The visitor holds a book in her lap in the leather chair, which fits like a glove, she'll tell the host later in a text message after her visit.

The host—truth be told—worries about the visitor alone in his house, who visits but doesn't leave to see sights or to do, well, anything.

The visitor intended to do many things while in the city. But then there was this warm, inviting kitchen and her friend living at the tippy-top of a hill that she's a tiny bit afraid to descend for no good reason and intimidated to walk up, and she didn't feel like leaving. She stares at the skyscraper tree, wondering what would happen if it toppled over.

The visitor has also taken to studying the big, fat, feral black-and-white cat that slinks around outside the window. Even with its swinging belly, the cat has a daintiness to it. Sniffing at this and pawing gently at that. The cat has class, or so the visitor has come to believe, as she studies it and the squirrels that scamper to and fro in search of something to improve their futures.

The traffic hums down below, so far away. The host, home from work now, turns the radio back on, paces the kitchen a few times, trying to get the visitor's attention. She does turn to look at him. A polite and civil person, she doesn't want to alarm him; it's just that she's so very tired. She wants to sit here without thinking about anything, no planning.

The host can't get his head around this and has gone out of his way to grab a local weekly paper that lists all of the fabulous events happening all the time, right down below them on the streets. The visitor smiles sweetly at this gesture and even looks carefully through the paper and circles everything that looks interesting to her. She sets the newspaper aside and then turns back to the road. The cat, the birds, the squirrels, the tree.

Finally the host suggests they walk around out there, in the world she's looking at. "How about a nice walk?" he says. She thinks that's a great idea. Not going down, just staying up above it all.

They'll walk the steep staircases that crisscross around his neighborhood. He'll dig out a guide that takes them higher and higher into unknown territory even for him until their thighs scream and they feel their lungs might break. The beautiful day suggests clarity, and all the critters and birds romping around them affirm it. They see no one else. The visitor is happy to be alone with the host. So happy she holds his hand as they walk along a flat stretch, past a tiny park with a swing set and a slide. She doesn't mean anything forward by the hand holding, and her host doesn't take it that way. Too much water under the bridge, he thinks, for such a little thing to spark a controversy in their friendship. The host is happy now. He's shown her something, at least, of his life.

The visitor's cheeks have flushed, her lungs are filled with fresh air, the sun and wind and the sheer height of it all as they step back into the house. The host knows she'll go straight to the chair. The world repeats itself like that. Everything resettles back where it began.

***

He sets a glass of wine near her elbow, the sun now sliding down behind the tall tree. "I love you," she says. Maybe it's too much. A little too close to something that once might have been.

"I love you, too," the host says, as he walks up the stairs toward his study, thinking he can get some work done while she's preoccupied with the tree and the view.

Soon pitch black swipes the tree away, and the visitor stares at her face in the big bare window's reflection, at her lips as she sips the red wine that the host set on a coaster within arm's reach. She sips but doesn't like the way her lips pucker toward the glass's rim, too eager.

The radio whispers into the night. The visitor is ready now to do something—to have an experience. Something surprising and life changing. She pulls the blind, finishes her glass of wine, and walks up the stairs toward the study. As she ascends, she unclasps her bra and lets it drop behind her. She can hear the host typing, a tiny rainstorm in the other room.

THE BEAR PLAYS BASKETBALL

Nancy Jones fears she has broken herself. Alone late one night, she thinks it through. The moon spotlighting the floor, the Christmas cactus no longer in bloom. She taps the windowsill—three, four, five times. She walks down the stairs, away from the bedroom, past the skeleton couch and chairs crouched in the living room, and out the back door onto the stiff, cold lawn.

Her nightgown ruffles her knees as the wind picks up. Nancy can't remember the last time she stood outside alone in the dead of night. That's how broken she is. She curtsies to the oak tree, the moon supervising.

"Well, what the fuck," she says to the night.

She's up a slight hill, beside the oak. The yard levels out at the top with a patio. Here she pitches forward a bit, turns to face the city. It could be any city, really—to her, at least. Tall buildings, lights, slow-moving traffic, neon, helicopters.

With her sense of direction? She could be anywhere. Tell her somewhere and she'd believe it. Detroit. Pittsburgh. Cincinnati.

The sloped yard rises up from the silent, dead-end street. Gauzy streetlights cast a yellow glow up and down the rows of houses. Nancy imagines their buzz, which she can't hear from here. And there in the flickering light is a six-foot-tall bear in a blue suit and matching hat, walking down the street. She holds her breath. The bear has a jaunty gait. A sort of jocky clip to each step, like it knows its way around a basketball court. Bear ears, bear snout—looking dapper.

But no, it isn't a bear turning onto the walkway to their house. It's Jimmy. Of course. Nice suit, former jock—crisp shirt even at this late hour, still tucked in.

Jimmy turns his key in the lock, and Nancy watches the kitchen light leak out the side window.

Once inside, she tries her mouthiness out on him. "What the fuck?" she says in the doorway.

Jimmy—with his snout already rooting through a ham sandwich—perks his ears; his broad shoulders freeze.

"What the fuck, Nancy," he says. "You scared the shit out of me. What're you doing up? Were you outside?" He sets his sandwich down on the counter, wipes his lips with a paper towel.

"I'm an opossum," she says, opening the fridge, pushing containers around until she finds the yogurt.

"Okay," Jimmy says. He rips a second paper towel from the roll, holds it under his chin as he begins to chew again, staring at her. Jimmy has deep stares. "Shouldn't you be playing dead, then?" he says.

"Or eating ticks," Nancy says, rummaging through the drawer for a spoon. "I eat a lot of ticks."

Jimmy takes this news earnestly, as he takes all news. "Or yogurt, apparently," he says.

"Right," Nancy says spooning the creamy goop right from the container into her mouth. "Alexa," she says, "play that opossum song."

And without missing a beat Alexa belts out some crazy psychedelic noise.

"Alexa, shut the fuck up," Jimmy says. And Alexa does. She shuts the fuck up. Everyone is impressed and quiet now. Nancy's nightgown glows in the bright kitchen light. Jimmy pulls his tie, unbuttons his shirt.

Nancy is not usually part of this ritual. Early to bed, early up. That's Nancy.

Not tonight.

Tonight, she knows that somewhere in this city that might as well be Denver or Boston there's a clean-cut bear strolling down the street, heading toward the moonlight, thinking bear thoughts, waiting for the next pickup basketball game.

The bear turns the corner, leaves these two to their own thoughts and games and ham sandwiches and yogurt. A dog barks in the distance. An opossum snuffles ticks in the backyard, a little vacuum cleaner humming a psychedelic tune, every so often looking up at the moon as if it holds some answers.

PHOTOS

Teresa pushes the box of old photographs a little farther along the table, toward the end closest to the door. Later, she'll carry it to the garbage can and just toss it in. Goodbye past, goodbye.

The radio babbles contemporary political debates. Today, immigration. Soon, it will switch to student protests. The day out there waits for her. Teresa wants to dive into it.

As she ties her walking shoes, her little dog, Ace, runs in circles, gleeful to go, but then hesitant. He's weird that way. Wanting to walk but then suddenly reluctant. The non-walk dog walk is Teresa's least favorite thing to do, but still, she loves Ace so she encourages him every few feet. "A walk! Look! We're going on a walk!" Giving a kind of play-by-play commentary to engage him in his here and now.

The dog had stayed up late, tossing and turning on his dog bed, wedged beside her bed, while she tossed and turned, and her lover tossed and turned and checked the clock every few minutes. Teresa knew he thought she couldn't see him checking. Longing to leave, she guessed. Longing to make too much noise leaving so he'd wake her and then say he didn't mean to, sorry. Who knew what went on in his head these days. His thoughts sometimes straightened out and he manifested into a great guy, and other times he was unreachable and mangled up and she couldn't understand him.

No one slept well last night, and all Teresa can muster the energy to do after the non-walk is stare into the bottom of her empty coffee cup. She'll fill it up soon. It's going to be a long day.

The clouds float by with certainty—moving on, quietly. Everything moving on, serving as some kind of example she can't decode as she contemplates the weight of the photos on her table and knows she has less and less time to get ready for work. Surely, there are a few good photos in the box. Snapshots of another life and time. The world bright and blue and focused in all the right places.

But paper photos can't be edited or cropped or Photoshopped. The world just doesn't have to be as half-assed as it once was. Teresa scrolls through the recent photos on her phone, a dizzy diary of food and flowers and a reluctant dog. There's her lover, the one who walked out the door earlier, a selfie snuck onto her phone the night before, deletable.

PARADISE

The bear had always wanted a piano. Or maybe not *always*, but then when he wanted one the urge came on as a long-suppressed desire, which made the longing deeper and longer.

Practically, he couldn't own a piano, but he could claim a few on his circuit. One near a sliding glass door never locked, one on a loading dock where that weird artist lived.

Timing is everything when you're a bear and not wanting to be caught, not wanting the spotlight, but needing some joy.

He played softly, working his way through a practice book. Scales and "Joy to the World." "Twinkle, Twinkle Little Star."

The music curled like waves through him and satisfied his broken heart. Mended it, really. Eventually.

There were moments late at night when, embraced by the base of his tree, smooth bark sturdy against his back—a kind of lifeline, that tree—he could move his paws, following the imaginary notes. Movement and song and silence all one. Then he felt full, whole, like a bear in paradise.

PROGRESS

Martha drank her coffee black. One cup a day. Today, in her T-shirt and jeans, she watched the trees sway outside her window. The screen's cross-hatched pattern softened the crisp spring greens, sharp browns, and the blue sky over her town. The river tumbled nearby, and, if followed, led to the city where she worked Monday, Wednesday, and Friday for a design firm in a sturdy building made of glass and granite, with an elevator that chirped pleasantly at each floor. Up, up, up, as Martha secured a smile onto her face. The doors opened at the fourth floor and she stepped forward to greet her coworkers, who offered her coffee that she refused and who said hello but probably didn't like her very much, a part-timer after all.

Because today was not a workday, Martha could frown into her coffee cup, absently mess with some callouses on her left foot, pet her dachshund, Pogo.

She needed to make a phone call that involved fixing some things on the other end of the line, smoothing out the family problems that had started months before. Her brother Sam. His not-girlfriend. Their mother. Everything getting muddy over the holidays. Her mother's feelings hurt (or so she said), and Sam saying that their mother liked to claim hurt feelings in order to hurt other people's feelings but indeed, her feelings couldn't actually be hurt—as Martha might well remember—because their mother had no feelings at all.

Martha sipped her coffee, now tepid, trying to calm the rising tension in her stomach. She stretched, and Pogo sat up from his little bed, eyeing her sneakers near the door. If Martha slipped on the sneakers, he would bark and run in circles and demand a walk; if she didn't—well—he didn't care what Martha did. *Me, me, me.* Pogo's way. Martha slipped on one shoe, Pogo stood, tipped his head, an ear flapped awkwardly the wrong way. Martha slid her foot out of the shoe. Pogo sat. "Lower your expectations," Martha said. "Remember, low expectations equal less disappointment."

She searched for her cell phone: sunroom, kitchen, bedroom. Pogo trailed behind, cautious, but soon distracted by a once-forgotten dog toy wedged in the corner of the pantry. Its squeaking became the background for Martha's conversation with her mother that morning. She began with hello, of course, and then broke right into a fast trot. "Remember to lower your expectations, Mom," she said. "Lower your expectations of what I'm about to say, and we'll move along just fine." Squeak.

"Don't be ridiculous," her mother said. Squeak. "I have no expectations for you. When are you coming to visit?" Squeak.

After a nearly unproductive talk, where Martha agreed, yes, Sam had gotten out of hand at Christmas dinner, but also confessed that she knew he'd been out drinking beforehand at O'Shea's, and, gradually, made her mother admit that she had insulted his now ex-girlfriend in real time, Martha hung up the phone, not feeling better but pleased at having checked something off her list. She'd see her brother later today and try to talk to him like an adult, even though their relationship had fossilized at an adolescent stage, which devolved into bickering and crude jokes every time they came face to face. Sam's fault. His track star status and good looks kept him trapped back in high school, mentally. He wanted a girl and fashionable clothes and a local bar with craft beer. He wanted to play darts or pool or pinball and tease his little sister and talk about the ladies he had failed with that month. The Girlfriends. It was a circle they traced in their conversations, cautiously sidestepping issues that needed tending. Their mother, what to do about her? But they didn't usually get to that conversation until they were drunk, and then—well—nothing good came of it all.

Martha put her sneakers on for real. Pogo waited for the leash to be snapped, acquiescing to the rules of this dog/owner game, willing to submit as long as he got his walk. Martha took long strides out into the breezy day. She needed fresh air and the river to calm her head.

Pogo liked to snuffle around without being interrupted by the big labs and retrievers popular in her neighborhood these days, so they took the skinny path down to the river's edge rather than the paved one that the regular walkers used.

As she rounded a muddy corner, talking full throttle at Pogo about her difficult mother, a young fisherman popped into view near the water. A familiar shadowed profile, but still, and for a moment, Martha paused, alone on this windy, chilly river path at 10:30 a.m. on a Thursday morning. *I'm tall and intimidating with good lungs*, she reminded herself. Her mother had once described her this way. And Pogo, always the neurotic pup, let out one of his howling yelps, running in circles, never discrete. The man, fishing, flipped up his jacket collar and tried—it seemed to Martha—to sink deeper into himself so he wouldn't have to look up or talk to her. He squatted down to sit on his haunches, his thin pole tucked under his arm, his line dangling in the water.

Martha snapped on her fourth-floor work smile and said, "Hello! Nice day. Catch anything?" She grabbed at the collar of her own jacket, waved a hand in his direction.

The man didn't turn to her, apparently uninterested in the role of friendly coworker. He lowered his thick eyebrows, got a better grip on the pole and mumbled, "I know who you are."

Martha let Pogo tug her farther along the path, yelled back, "Oh, you do—do you?" She mumbled to herself, "Some days I wonder who I am myself, so that's pretty impressive."

"Don't push it," the man said. His tone made Martha a tiny bit furious instead of disturbed because she'd talked to her mother on the phone earlier and she needed to vent her pent-up energy somewhere. But still, she kept walking, working off the steam the world too often pressurized inside her.

"Fuck off," she said after a while, not that loud. Pogo snuffled up the bank. When she looked back the guy was far off in the distance, but she could have sworn he smiled as he recast his line.

They made a big loop back to her front stoop, the emotional residue of the fishing man sticking to her like glue, Pogo and her sneakers caked with mud. Martha plopped her shoes on the welcome mat and picked up the dog, smearing what now seemed like clay all over her windbreaker. Pogo let his feet hang limp, resolved for the bath that he knew followed his joy. "Pleasure and pain," Martha said to him. "That's what we deal with here on this Earth. You get the crazy muddy walk and then you get the horrible bath. That's the pact we've struck. You know this. I don't want any whining."

Pogo whined and squirmed all through the bath. Martha shammied him off with a towel and he soon chewed on a bone in his tiny bed. Martha herself cleaned the stove top and then sliced potatoes that she would roast and eat standing up at the window.

Later, as she slid just one more salty fried wedge into her mouth, chewing and considering the shagginess of her front lawn, the man from the river trudged by, his pole over his shoulder, his gait heavy with work boots and his denim jacket. He held a paper bag in his left hand and swung it slightly with each step. "I know who you are," Martha said. Yeah, right. She'd keep an eye out for Mr. Fisherman. He turned onto Pleasant Avenue, walking down the middle of the street. *Get along, Mr. Cowboy*, Martha thought. *Get along.*

A text from Sam: "Call me." By which he meant text him. She called her friend Sylvia instead. Sylvia hated to be interrupted at work, but Martha couldn't help herself some days. Sylvia answered, already annoyed.

"Hello, dear," Martha said. "Do you know me?"

Sylvia said, "Yes." And started to say something else with a tone of explanation.

"Thank you," Martha said, trying to stop her. "I don't know why I called you. Please stop being annoyed with me. A burly dude with a fishing pole said he knew me, which I know isn't true, then he walked by my house, and I just called you for a little check-in, okay?"

"Okay." Sylvia softened a little. "I have to go, Martha."

***

Martha's mother had always dressed little Martha in outfits. Matching socks and shorts and shirts. Crisp polyester. Colorful and itchy. The bows in her hair complementing everything. Then she sat her in the sunroom to play. Once there Martha felt like she might break if she did anything wrong.

Martha lined up her stuffed animals. Their eyes asked questions, like, *Are you our mother?* She admitted to the animals, that yes, she'd been assigned to them. She would take care of them, see? Here's a plastic bottle to drink from. Here's a little dress to wear. Now just sit there and try not to break. She rearranged the order of the bears and dogs and kittens and then rearranged it again. Eventually, she imagined them all onto a boat in the middle of the sea. Martha tucked her feet up onto the couch, an arm curled around as many as she could fit. They drifted. Martha assured everyone they would be fine.

While she drifted, Sam blurred by the window, shirtless and running. Sam, sweat and tube socks. Some days they tried to play together, but she almost always cried at the end, running to tell on him to her mother. He had turned the hose on her full blast or tripped her or helped her up into the big front yard maple and then wouldn't get her down. Exhausting for Martha. Her mother patient back then, if distant. Soft, warm food smells floating through the house. The sound of an iron hissing at her father's work shirts, smoothed flat and then onto a wire hanger, lined up on a collapsible rack. White, white, white, blue.

Although Martha had lived her entire life with her father, each time he came through the front door after his workday, a kind of trepidation spread up from her spine. What did she fear? His presence. His certainty. His expectation that she would have answers to his questions. That right and wrong answers existed and she didn't know the difference. She loved and feared her father, who wore those hiss-pressed clean shirts and a tie and pants with pockets that jingled with change. She said the wrong things and he re-asked the questions and she said the right things. In this way, she came to understand what to say.

***

Sam set his empty coffee cup on the windowsill. His small apartment had many windows—the sills all lined with rocks, corks, empty wine bottles converted to candle holders, shells, buttons, matchbooks, marbles, and mugs in which often floated little colorful clouds of mold. Sam liked piles, but his dates—if they got as far as his apartment—didn't appreciate the chaos. He refused to change, thought the right person would understand the mess, would perhaps help him.

Suzy, the bright blonde he'd gone out with last month, said his place looked like an archaeological dig. She wouldn't set down her purse, kept it clutched to her side while she sipped the glass of wine he'd poured for her. Someone at the office had set them up—maybe Mac?—said Suzy worked at the law firm around the corner, thought they'd be a good fit, said she used big words like Sam did. He had a good time that night. A good dancer, Suzy. Great smile, funny. She said he was a one-of-a-kind person—the kind of person she liked—until the apartment. Small, cramped, and cluttered.

Today, Sam made a point of grabbing his mug from the sill. He carried it to the sink and rinsed it out to impress the invisible future judgers. He set it in the drying rack. "So there," he said.

Sam had plans to meet his sister Martha. She had ideas she needed to bounce off him. He had become a kind of walking process journal for her. Instead of scribbling her innermost thoughts into a diary, she scheduled late brunch with him. He didn't know what to think of it. What did he know about life? About love? What did he know about anything? He did like taking a personal day off from work, though.

He ran his fingers through his short hair, pecking at it with his fingers to get it to lay flat, but not too flat. He put on a nice shirt—the shirt that Martha liked so she'd compliment it first thing and make him feel good and handsome. Sam pulled on jeans, sneakers, an easy day. No big thoughts haunting his head, except for the memory of Suzy in the pink dress with the clutch purse, great dancer. She'd touched his arm and smiled before they made it to his place. She had ideas.

"Dashed dreams," he said, melodramatically. He liked to say these kinds of things out loud. He'd start his brunch conversation with Martha this way.

***

They arrived at the exact same time at Cous-Cous by the River. Martha made a wave of her hand and said, "Smooth."

"Dork," Sam said. He put his arm through hers. Sometimes people thought they were a couple and sometimes this made both of them feel better.

The waitress looked at them skeptically. "Drinks?" she said.

"Of course," Sam said.

"I thought so," the waitress said.

"Bloody Marys," Martha said. "Isn't that why everyone comes here?"

The waitress, the chef's niece, said, "Not everyone. Some people love the food." She held her head very still, practiced a look of condescension that she would perfect in her thirties when she owned a restaurant of her own that was exclusive and over-priced and perched above the New England seashore.

For now, she worked in this small city, at a place along the river—not the ocean by any stretch, she knew; she could feel its inferiority—and bided her time. She'd learn what she could from her uncle and then criticize him and his ways. After he died, many years from now, and the waitress hit her fifties and softened and learned—after many hardships—how to be decent, she would praise him, credit him with teaching her discipline and kindness before she knew what to do with them.

She sighed. "Two Bloody Marys, then?" Just to make her position clear, to give them one more chance at redemption.

"To start, yes," Martha said, and then Martha and Sam ignored her, too eager to begin talking to worry about her opinion of their drink orders.

"Dashed dreams," Sam said as the server walked away.

"Here we go again," Martha said. Sam and Martha nodded at each other. Soon they carried their vodka-ed tomato juice to the fix-it-yourself bar in the corner of the place. There they adorned and enhanced their drinks. A celery stalk, some olives, capers, hot sauce, a lemon, a few cold shrimp, hot pickled peppers. Martha's drink tasteful—well-balanced, with a toothpick alternating olive/shrimp/olive, a lemon slice on the side, while Sam created a nightmare concoction with three sticks and barely room for his lips to sneak in and take a taste.

"Nice one," Martha said. "The waitress is going to love that."

"Dashed dreams," Sam said again. "Dashed dreams, my friend." And they clinked glasses, settled into their chairs, fingered the paper menu that held Thursday's lunch specials, finally ready to order some food.

***

One day, around the time Martha turned six years old, something happened that changed the way she made decisions for the rest of her life. She was playing games at the neighbor's house, a big group of kids running and screaming, playing Bloody Murder and Hide and Seek. They ran in swarms like gnats rising and falling over a river. The older kids—Marie and Danny—tried to explain the rules to play a proper game with people being "it" and "out." But the younger, slower kids let the boundaries lapse, came out of hiding too soon, ran in circles screaming for no reason, cried when they couldn't run fast enough to tag.

Martha wore her matching shorts set, her hair in two long ponytails, tinier than everyone else, in impractical sandals instead of sneakers. The games always seemed unfair. In later years, grown up, she would realize—they *were* unfair. She had been right. She felt ridiculous for remembering such things, holding grudges against her childhood.

Soon Martha and the neighbor kids were playing horse, running in big romping circles, and someone had a lasso. Someone had gotten a plastic cowboy hat as a present, and a parent had offered up a pile of handkerchiefs for the bandits. Martha had a big red bandanna around her neck and liked this game very much because the rules remained ambiguous and running wild in circles seemed like just the thing to do on a summer day.

At some point an older boy showed up. Not unusual to have another kid join in, since the neighborhood teemed with children who broke into a variety of sets and subsets as the day wore on. Some came out of the woodwork just to join in a baseball game, others to pile into a car for a trip to the nearby amusement park. This new boy wore tight, faded Wrangler jeans, a little worn at the knees, and Converse shoes and white socks. He had on a T-shirt, once dark blue and now a matte gray, the collar a little worn. His lanky hair ran down to his shoulders and his glasses had thick brown plastic frames. A bit hokey. A bit loopier and looser than the rest, but he teased and made jokes with everyone and soon fit in.

Yet, no one seemed to know him, and some of the kids shied away naturally. But Martha had a magnet, a force that drew people in, would draw people in for years to come, and the boy singled her out right away. Her cute pink shorts and white shirt with a pink plaid elephant on the front. Her brown sandals with short wooden heels that she unstrapped and threw to the side as she romped in the circle, wanting to be a horse, wanting to become a horse, to play horse forever. She loved this game. They all practiced neighing.

Eventually they ran through the paths in the woods instead of in the big front lawn. Narrow paths that they sledded on in the winter months, still packed with dead leaves—the smell of mold and earth and must all around. Dim light spread through the tree branches. In the woods the group splintered, some kids called home for lunch, others to chores or shopping. Martha heard her mother's call and ran to her back door. She lived in a much bigger house than her friends, but they hardly ever played there. No one knew why. "Where are your shoes?" is the first thing her mother asked, then, "Where did you get that scarf?" She straightened Martha's shirt and fixed her ponytails, untying the bandanna and wadding it into her palm.

"I left them over there," Martha pointed in the general direction of their play. "At that one girl's house? The one with the big eyes?" Here she widened her eyes. "We're playing cowboy."

"Don't do that with your eyes," her mother said. "Her name is Marie and you're a cowgirl." And then she fished in her shopping bag and gave Martha a present—a shiny plastic apple that was one-quarter eaten, strung on a leather string with a little mouse smiling from its side. Martha knew the other girls would be jealous and that a mother or two might make a comment about her being spoiled. Not the first or last comment about this. But Martha couldn't help what her mother did. She had no idea how to stop her. She had no idea that she should stop her until years later when it was too late.

She put on the necklace. Ran back to play some more, but by this time most of the kids had left, except for the new boy, leaning against a tree. "I've been waiting for you," he said.

"Do you want to play? Where is everybody?" Martha asked.

"I don't know, but I'll play with you," he said.

"What's your name?" Martha asked. She found her sandals, abandoned near the front stoop and strapped them back onto her filthy, grass-stained feet.

"Tim," he said. "C'mon, I want to show you something."

They walked through the woods. Tim keeping up an even banter. Teasing her and making jokes and even complimenting her new necklace. The sun started to slant and Martha knew her mother would soon call her in to get a bath and help set the table for dinner. She knew her brother would come home from baseball practice and they'd eat and watch TV together. She did these things every night.

Eventually, they walked into her own backyard, Martha and Tim. In later years, Martha would wonder if Tim knew it was hers, but how could he have known that? They'd taken the paths through the woods that ran across all the backyards and ended up here, near the grape arbor and the old shed they didn't use. Her father would eventually tear it down. This day the grapes hung heavy on their vines and the shed had a low roof and was situated on the bottom section of a slight hill. Tim, who was much taller, could lift her up and set her on the edge of the roof. Funny at first, he'd made some joke about holding her for ransom, some story about her being a princess cowgirl, about having to give up her new necklace to come down.

Just like Sam, he'd put her in a situation where she couldn't get down by herself. Pretty far from the ground and not that brave, the roof tiles like sandpaper on the backs of her legs, Martha felt a small tingling of fear that he would leave her there. "Give me a kiss and you can get down," Tim said.

And she said no, because she didn't want to give him a kiss. Stubborn and spoiled, she didn't have to do things she didn't want to. That had been her life until this point.

She scootched back a little. "Just one little kiss and you can go," Tim said. The thought that he might know her brother came to Martha then, Tim being older and putting her in this not-fun location. "Do you know my brother, Sam?" she said.

Tim said, "Yea, we know each other. We're friends." And somehow knowing this made things better. Easier to understand.

"I'm still not kissing you," she said.

Tim said, "What are you going to do then?"

And Martha knew what to say, what had always worked in the past. "I'm going to tell my mom."

Tim leaned back a little, crossed his arms over his faded T-shirt and said, "Go ahead."

And Martha yelled. She yelled, "Mom!" She yelled and when she was done silence washed in. She could just turn and barely see a speck of the shadowed kitchen window of her house. Did Tim know this was her house?

He said, "Go ahead. Yell again."

Martha yelled louder. She really yelled this time. And her mother did not come. Always, every time until this day, her mom had answered, had come to her side.

"She won't come," Tim said, "because she can't hear you."

And how could he have known that? Known that a little girl voice wouldn't travel up the slight hill, as the little girl sat with her back to the house, afraid to turn fully around because she might fall. Stuck on the roof of her own family's shed with a stranger, Sam's friend, a stranger who said, "Give me a kiss." The musty scent of the grapes heavy in the early evening humidity.

What happened next throbs at the edges of Martha's conscious thoughts, a muddy black sky in her memory. Face down in the weedy grass, her cheekbone pushed at dirt. Jumped? From the roof, maybe? Did she kiss him? She doesn't know. Alone and feeling splattered inside and out, she cried as she walked to her own back stoop, toward the blank window behind which dinner waited. Her necklace lost, gone.

***

Sam fidgeted with his napkin, slurped at his Bloody Mary. Martha outlined the issues with their mother, her poor treatment of Sam's last girlfriend, how her mother had grudgingly agreed not to talk about future girlfriends' bodies or hairstyles in front of them as if they weren't present. "Progress?" Martha said.

"Progress!" Sam said. "Maybe?"

They needed more drinks to be certain, but would this waitress even oblige?

"I can't stop thinking about Suzy. The way she danced and then how she basically deflated before my eyes after she saw my apartment. My stuff. My detritus," Sam said.

Martha nodded. "You do have a lot of things scattered all over your place. I think it was hard for Suzy—really any person but especially a date—to see how she could fit into your life. But if you're still stuck on her, give her a call. Wasn't she the lawyer? Mom will love her without complaint."

"I feel like they just need to accept me, you know? It's what I like. I mean, I dress nice. I shower. All the stuff—totally kept. Why can't I have my external crisis laid out for all to see?"

Martha didn't know why he couldn't do that. But neither of them was good at dating. Friends? Yes. Partners? No. "You have trust issues," she said, knowing that she had trust issues, too, but it was easier to say that than to try to get at the root of his collections, which had started around the time of their father's death. She wasn't going to mention that either. Death, dying, flying through the air, landing on her face. The guy today, fishing. He knew her. How?

"There was this guy today, fishing on the river," Martha said. "I think maybe he might be a friend of yours? Kind of rough Timberland boot flannel shirt type with a beard? He said he knew me. Kind of ominous. *I know you*, kind of thing. What's that about?" she said. Even as she said it she knew it couldn't be true. Years ago Tim had said he was Sam's friend and he wasn't; she knew that soon after, when they were driving with their mother to the grocery store and there was Tim loping along the sidewalk. "There's your friend!" Martha yelled as if Tim was a great guy. The connection electric. Sam dropped his jaw as he scanned the sidewalk from the passenger seat, having called shotgun. "What? Who? That weird guy? What are you talking about?" The car zipped by and the conversation shifted and Tim disappeared forever, forever unknown.

"Why do you always assume all these creepy guys you meet are my friends?" Sam asks. "It's the weirdest thing, like you see this semi-homeless looking person over by your office who asks you for money and you're like, 'Do you know this man who carries around a PBR tall boy in a bag?' Like when have I ever known people like this?" Sam stabbed some lettuce on his plate and snapped at it like a turtle, then jabbed his grilled salmon. "I want another drink," he said. "You are such a weirdo, Martha."

"Look, I talked to Mom for you about a stupid girlfriend you don't even have any more so you'll show up the next time she invites us and I won't have to go alone. I did that. So, I get to talk about this creepy fishing guy. How would he know me? How?"

Sam motioned to the server, who ignored him. He would soon stand up to get the manager, but for now he clutched at his water glass, slugged the water like whiskey. "Did you ever think that he's some kind of fucked-up predator? Super angry at women and is just, I don't know, completely fucking with you, Martha? Second question: Does he even exist or is he some manifestation of creepy-guy syndrome that you conjure, have conjured for some time in your small, small pea-sized brain? I do wonder about you spending so much time alone."

"Not pea-sized. Smarter than you, always," Martha said. "Governor's scholarship, remember?" Had she imagined the fisherman talking to her? She didn't think so, but this is how the world turned for her, this kind of questioning from far back to now at this brunch table. What happened?

Sam pushed his chair back, clutched his napkin and then threw it onto his chair's seat. He was off to find the manager.

Martha imagined the table floating out to sea. She wondered what it would be like to never make it back to shore, where Sam was still running in circles until she told on him and then he laughed and added to his piles. Their father gone, their mother a distant speck in the window.

THE DOG, AGAIN

The dog barks twice. Two quick yelps with his snout to the air.

The man says, "Bad. Dog." But he doesn't mean it. The man lies down on the floor and the dog jumps up on his chest as if to pin him there so he can't get away. The dog loves to play this game, his tongue out while he pants with pleasure at securing this man to the floor. It never lasts. The man will say something like, "All right then," and the dog knows it's over but will grumble and half growl in his way. The man sits up, stands up, and says, "Now, where was I," as the dog struts over to his little food bowl and crunches some kibble.

He then lies down like a good dog on his little pillow in the corner, and the man begins to type on his computer. The sun sinks low in the kitchen, where the man works, aglow with late fall. A pretty and nostalgic scene of man and dog. The man taps away, and soon the little dog snores.

The woman comes home bursting with grocery bags. A variety of mismatched canvas totes stuffed with produce and dried goods. She stopped at the co-op and shopped a big one—unlike the little ones she usually does—bulk items and whole grain pasta and cheeses and a splurge on some new local salted caramel ice cream. She hardly ever splurges.

"I'm here!" she says to the room, and the dog knows this is his cue to go ballistic with barking.

The man stops typing and looks up at her and smiles. "Help?" he asks.

"No, but hello," she says and travels her hoard over to the fridge. The bags sag on the floor, and after taking off her scarf, the woman digs in, putting everything in its proper place. This is her domain, and she likes to get it all put away, though she isn't necessarily neat at other times. "It's good to get a head start," she says.

The man nods and says, "MmmmHmmm," not really listening to her as he taps away at his keyboard. The dog barks a few more times for good measure, and they simultaneously tell him to be quiet now. He walks to his pillow like a little pugilist retiring to his corner of the ring.

The woman finishes her putting away, and now it's dusk, even though it isn't late. She thinks about dinner—what to make or where to go. The world has so much potential and she feels full of it today, bursting with all the stuff that has been done, that could be done. She paces around the kitchen, waits for a pause in the man's typing. When it comes, she says, "So?"

And he knows that his work time is nearly up because the only person more insistent than the dog is the woman when she's hungry. "Glass of wine?" he says.

She says, "Hmmmm." Now that she has his attention, she's not sure where she wants to take this night. The man's phone rings. It beeps and chirps and he answers it and shrugs at the woman.

He walks outside to talk and gesture in their little front yard as their neighbors walk by and wave and mouth hello to him. He talks and talks and now the woman, bored and impatient, wants to eat. She hates that she's like this, but she is. Jealous of a phone.

She taps on the glass of the picture window and raises two fingers, which means two minutes, and the man nods because he is aware of the rising jealousy and knows he needs to manage this the way he manages his office. He needs to get off the phone and pay some attention to the woman and everything will cool off.

The woman lets the dog outside and the dog races around the man and starts to bark. The man clicks off the phone and slides it into his back pocket. He pats the dog on the head and says, "Job done, mister." And with that, the dog runs back to the door, victorious.

The woman decides to roast potatoes, and she does want a glass of wine thank-you-very-much. Red wine—dark and peppery.

The potatoes start to sizzle and the man hands the woman the glass of wine, which he overfills because he believes in abundance. They tap glasses.

"I love you," she says. She doesn't say this very often, so they both pause to assess the terrain. "I really do," she says.

"I know," he says. "I do, too." They sit across from each other at the table with the little dog nestled on the floor at their feet, and light the candles. The man thinks, *We're a little family.* He has never thought this before, or never in this way exactly. Afraid to say it out loud, he wants to hold this idea close to his heart, let it stew for a while. He grabs her hand, rubs his thumb across the top of her knuckles. Little circles.

"We're gonna do it," she says, resting her hand on top of his like a warm blanket. Sometimes it seems like they aren't going to make it, but not today.

"Today is a great day," she says. "Tomorrow will be even better."

LUCK

Margo's long black hair was the first thing Owen noticed the day they met. The word came to him in an elegant font—*supernatural*—all lower case.

The design firm had sent him over to show the museum's Publications Committee the preliminary mock-ups for the exhibition invitation. Owen, a good front person for the firm. Young, handsome, fashionable, but without much ego and a little naive. He agreed to nod and agree even if he didn't agree. Rumor at the firm was the museum's eccentric director, Mr. Dirk, had unpredictable tastes and that the committee itself no longer had opinions but instead tried to channel Dirk's, which led to some heated and nearly surreal debates very much like séances. Owen had been told that under no circumstances was he to laugh out loud during the discussion. His firm wanted to keep this account, and others had been fired for less reason.

"No sarcasm, Owen," his boss Caroline said, stopping by his cubicle with the final mock-ups, brushing invisible lint off his jacket collar. "Honestly. Be cute and smart but not snotty, okay?"

"Cute not snotty. Smart. Got it, Caroline," Owen said. He wondered if he had a reputation for snottiness or if Caroline was in a mood. He felt slightly paranoid and queasy. She tapped his desk twice before disappearing down the hall.

***

Margo, the museum's curator, had thick lips, expertly covered in burgundy-toned lipstick that complemented her sage green jacket, her trim black skirt. Owen appreciated fine clothes, and after introducing himself and declining tea, coffee, and water, he said, "Your jacket perfectly accents your hair."

Owen liked when colors worked in the world—by accident or on purpose—and enjoyed telling people so, pointing them out.

"I'm glad you approve, Owen. Often, I need a man's approval before I can begin my day," Margo said. She smiled, just slightly, a smug smirk that suggested she had a graduate degree in art history from Columbia.

Owen smiled; he imagined the words into small rubber chickens bouncing off him. "It's the shade of green that works," he continued, "any darker and it would just make your hair fall into the background."

Other members of the committee filed in, looking burdened and pasty as they swiveled into their seats clutching travel mugs and ceramic mugs and one 32 oz. clear plastic water bottle with the ounce demarcations lining its side like a ruler.

Owen held up the three designs, neatly tacked onto black poster board, one at a time, talking through the positive aspects of each. Bold title; a style showcasing the exhibition's signature image; conceptual approach. He smiled as earnestly as he possibly could without looking fake. When he held up the last example, flipping it forward from face down on the table like a giant flashcard, the previously lethargic group gasped. Owen stopped his prepared speech, looked to make sure he'd brought the right card. This design featured the conceptual idea (his idea)—a red square that simply said "Art" in the center in black Helvetica and then, in tiny print on the right, below, "invite." All the information and images would be inside the card, a surprise from such a stuffy institution—although he did not say that out loud.

"What?" Owen said, slightly unprofessional, but he couldn't ignore the faces turned to him that looked, if he had to guess, mortified.

The committee—two men, three women, all wearing fitted black, gray, or slate pants, skirts, shirts, and jackets—skittled a little in their seats. One man rolled his eyes, laughed, and leaned back in his chair.

"Dirk doesn't permit red," Margo finally said after clearing her throat, tapping the end of her pen on the table.

"Of course," Owen said, smiling. He flipped the card face down, pushed at it, wishing it to fall through the table and disappear. "Dirk.

No red," he said and then wondered if that was snotty as he turned back to the other two options.

After haggling over the font choice and size, the copy's specific wording, whether the image had or had not been cropped—Owen was reminded by the committee that there was no cropping of the image under any circumstances—the assembled museum employees did what Owen had been advised they would do: designed by committee. They agreed on a square card with the title at the top, the image below ("uncropped, with the proper citation") and the rest of the invitation text inside with the new ("not the old") logo. The card stock itself would be heavy ("but not too heavy, remember what happened last year with the Daumier show") and sage green, nearly the color of Margo's jacket.

Margo walked Owen down the narrow tile hallway and into the bright afternoon light. Stark white clouds puttered across a sheer blue sky. The air itself seemed astonishing to Owen. He took a deep breath, thankful to be alive and no longer in that meeting. Margo continued with him to the parking lot. She took stiff, brisk strides. He sensed this kind of escort might be required by the employee handbook and not offered out of kindness or with carefree spontaneity. Margo looked straight ahead and not at him, the line of her profile stunning. Owen wanted to trace it with his fingertip—or sketch her quickly in the notebook he always kept in his bag.

Owen stopped beside his Nissan, not shabby, but red. "Dirk wouldn't approve," Owen said, deadpan, pressing the unlock icon on his fob.

"What?" Margo said. She turned to face him. Looked at his getaway car resting there beside the center island landscaping, looked at Owen. "No," she said. "Seriously. He would not. You have no idea what you're talking about."

She raised her thin hand to him, and he nearly kissed it like royalty because he thought that would be protocol, but realized it was just that Margot didn't shake well. He took her limp fingers and waggled them. Bowed to her, because it seemed appropriate, got into his car, whacked his door closed, and thanked his lucky stars that he got to drive back to his little firm, whose offices were cozy and pleasant, with a whole spectrum of colors and a nice kitchen area where he had deposited some freshly baked apple-walnut muffins that morning. His coworkers, friendly and secure for the most part in their positions and their design skills, would leave him a muffin to be nice, even if they wanted to eat them all.

The people in the office liked Owen, despite the fact he was a little prim and rarely joined them for happy hour cocktails at the fancy bar just down the street. They felt a kind of pity for him; they didn't know why, but everyone worked together to protect Owen from disappointment. They rallied around him, and Owen stayed there even though he'd already gotten offers from bigger, better firms. He liked Joan and Mark and Doug and Kendra. Honestly. Without footnotes. And his boss, Caroline, hardly ever messed with him.

***

A few weeks later, the exhibition invitations hit mailboxes. RSVPs received and noted. As the opening event at the museum neared, Owen's firm suggested he attend with the complimentary invite they'd received. He'd told them the story of the committee's rejection of the color red, and Kendra dared him to go dressed in red from head to toe. Or, if that was too much, just in red shoes or carrying a red square that he could flash Dirk's way to see what happened. Owen said he'd go. "Why not," he said. "Free food." They all agreed.

He thought about Margo, wondered what she'd be like without the lipstick, in dark blue sweats and a yellow T-shirt, fast walking around a green track.

The night of the opening, Owen ironed his dress shirt (soft white, 100 percent cotton) and his trousers (black, trim, flat front) and picked a dark gray suit jacket his mother had given him last Christmas. As an afterthought, he tucked a neatly folded silk handkerchief in its front pocket. A rich red, not a shabby primary, but a really nice, well-thought-out red that had some blue behind it and leaned toward maroon but didn't get there. Owen thought it would make a good story at the office on Monday. The handkerchief had been his father's. Nervous to take it out of his cottage, he hesitated at the front door, then stepped broadly, purposely out to the landing. He patted the handkerchief to make sure it stayed in placc.

Owen's father had died when he was very young, and his eccentric, antique-collecting mother had raised him, coddled him, imbued him with a vibe that made people want to shelter Owen his whole adult life. He longed for his father in a way some people longed for happiness or peace. His dad was a concept he carried around, usually only inside his small cottage. Tonight would be different. His dad would attend a fancy art opening.

The museum bustled with people Owen had never seen on the streets of their town. They seemed fragile and imported. Everything breakable: the delicate puffed appetizers lined with chopped shrimp, the hesitant line drawings on the walls, the stem glasses filled with pinot grigio. Owen located Margo standing in the corner with another of the committee members. He smiled and walked their way, holding his stem glass carefully. He took a sip.

"Hello," Owen said.

Margo looked up, startled, like a heron or some other long-legged bird wading in water. "Hello, Henry," she said. Her beautiful natural-fiber pant suit offset her hair well, but Owen decided not to point that out.

"Owen," he corrected.

Margo spotted his handkerchief, her eyes riveted to his chest for just a second. Then, her prim demeanor changed to bubbling. Bubbling at someone just over Owen's right shoulder. Bubbling like an old-time water cooler. "Mr. Dirk, hello. I'd like for you to meet our designer for the exhibition's invitation. His name is Henri." She pronounced it now with a French accent. Margo then looked at Owen like he was a special long-lost guest who held a life preserver in his arms, having just returned from the sea. "Henri, this is the museum's executive director and curator of this exquisite show, Mr. Dirk."

Owen's glass tapped against Mr. Dirk's as he turned. Nothing spilled. It was a clink really, like the end of a satisfying toast. Owen nodded, tipped his glass in Dirk's direction. "Congratulations," he said. Mr. Dirk wore a brown tweed suit. He seemed sculpted and moneyed and smart in a waxy Ivy League way. Owen could read all this just by the way he held his wine glass. Anyone could. His spectacles glinted in the museum lobby's light. "Exhibition, not show," he directed to Margo. "Please call me Dirk," he said, bemused, to Owen.

Owen noticed Margo now beamed like a kindergartener who'd just been happily reprimanded for messing up an alphabet recitation.

"Beautiful show, Dirk," Owen said. They stood in an awkward silence for one, two seconds. "Why no red?" No forethought for this question, his hanky egged him on, throbbing at this chest.

Margo gasped quietly but audibly, put her thin hand to her face and immediately shifted that gesture into a look of intellectual concern. Owen kept his face expressionless, as Dirk frowned and took a sip of wine, paused to reflect. The handkerchief gave a little wave from Owen's chest, a beacon. "Did you hear about that tulip nonsense? Gaudy miscommunication from the bottom up," he finally said. "A real fiasco. But needed. Surely you understand the importance of color and symmetry, being what you are, if you are, really, a designer?" Dirk smiled blandly, looked over Owen's shoulder, readying for his next target.

Owen said thank you. He stepped to the side to encourage Dirk's mingling. Dirk strode away without saying goodbye.

The next week Owen asked Margo over for dinner. That she said yes was a surprise to everyone involved.

***

Gene and Jolene, quiet literature and history professors at the local university, lived in the big house in front of Owen's cottage. They loved gardening in their spare time, and Owen baked them cookies during finals week and sometimes stopped in at their parties, bringing a tasteful bottle of wine or cognac. The cottage had a separate driveway that curved off the back alley. Owen parked his Nissan there. In the spring and summer, he grew herbs in the window boxes on the two front windows—rosemary, tarragon, oregano, and marjoram. Gene and Jolene gave him veggies from their garden.

He'd rented this cottage as a college student. Back then, he owned a ratty couch, his childhood desk with a lamp on it, and a bed. He drank cheap whiskey and wrote bad poetry on a manual typewriter, tossing his poems into the trashcan as quickly as he composed them, embarrassed to show the world the chaos inside his head. *Clack-clack, clack-ding*. He remembered his strong fingers pounding away to that chorus. The train's whistle across town. That and the desperate squirrels scampering across his roof loaded with acorns, a loose one tap-tap-tapping to the ground.

In those days, he often felt like he was waiting for his life to collapse in upon itself. But it didn't collapse—or he survived—and he decided to get a degree in graphic design instead of flunking out of English Lit. He chose to love colors forever one day in May when the morning sky unveiled itself in glorious blue and the whitest, cleanest clouds sailed by his window like sailboats. The sun shifted through the clouds and the young leaves shouted in kelly green—the forsythia blooming like butter down the alleyway.

He just couldn't leave this little place, even though he now made enough money to afford a big house on the better side of town, even though most of his friends had moved on to big cities. When Gene and Jolene offered to sell it to him, he said yes. When his mother asked why, he told her he opted for quality over quantity. He told her he liked continuity.

Now, a leather couch and matching armchair and ottoman—a rich deep brown with hints of auburn—anchored the front room. It had taken Owen a while to find the right set. A refurbished antique stand-up lamp with a tangerine orange glass globe on top—tiny flowers etched along its rim—a present from his mother after she accepted that he would probably live in this house forever. A glass coffee table, thick with art books stacked on top and beneath. A small hunter green enameled woodburning stove with a basket for kindling at its side where a fireplace had once been. Hardwood floors and a Persian rug his mother had salvaged from her own mother's house years before. Thick white pillar candles shrouded by tall glass globes lined the mantel. The main living space had just enough room for this and his small desk and chair. A wooden bar with stools was built into the wall separating the living room from the kitchen. Teal blue trim and cupboards with white walls in the kitchen. A magnetic strip held an array of Henkel knives and a pegboard wall hung his collection of La Creuset pans in orange, yellow, and blue. A deep enamel sink with a drainboard. The black-and-white checkered floor made Owen's heart purr. He had installed it himself.

Other than a small bathroom with a clawfoot tub and a back laundry room that led to the back door, that layout made up his whole first floor. Hooks on the walls in the living room for coats in the winter, a raincoat in the spring, garden tools in the summer. Hooks in the kitchen for an apron and canvas shopping bags. Up a narrow staircase that folded in upon itself was a loft that held Owen's bed, a closet, dresser, and a window with a fine view of the rolling hills that skirted the river outside town. A trunk at the end of the bed held extra blankets, sweaters, his sketches. Here he had a clock radio. Downstairs, on a tiny stool by the front door, was a boom box. He hadn't owned a TV in years.

Owen had always imagined a big, bustling home instead of the small, silent one he grew up in, but sometimes a person doesn't know what he wants until he finds it. So, he luxuriated in staying.

***

A glug of olive oil, the sting of onion mellowing toward caramel. The heady scent of garlic. Familiar smells that started nearly each meal Owen cooked. He chopped the half pound of mushrooms quickly, his knife rocking with precision on his cutting board. He swiped them into a big bowl, diced some celery, and threw the ends of the vegetables into the stock pot he had bubbling on the back of the stove. Once the onions gained translucence, slippery with oil, he tossed in the mushrooms, which made a slithering hiss. He put a lid on the pan, turned down the flame.

He had decided to try a new recipe for Margo, a mushroom cassoulet that looked creamy and comforting in the cookbook's photograph. He lifted the lid—earthy steam rose into the kitchen—added some fresh tarragon, a dash of thyme. He had bread dough rising in a bowl. He would make rosemary baguettes and a fresh green salad with sunflower seeds and pears, roasted walnuts, and a lemon vinaigrette dressing.

After punching down the puff of dough, he snaked out baguettes, taking off his watch and rolling up his sleeves before digging in. He rested the two rising loaves on his cookie sheet dusted with cornmeal, made cross-hatched slash marks on their tops, covered them with a dish towel. Checked the time. The flowers, an impulse buy from the grocery store, sagged listlessly in a mason jar. Some daisies with baby's breath that he'd picked out and thrown away. Nothing he could do about it, so he tied the red silk handkerchief around the jar's rim.

Owen stirred the mushrooms, which had started to release their meaty juices, checked his stock, greased an oven dish with a swish of olive oil, and combined everything with some cream, breadcrumbs on top, and slid it and the baguettes into the oven while he started on the apple tart.

He turned up the music, Mozart, concentrated on peeling away the apple skins. He sliced the apples paper thin, fanned them on top of the delicate spread of custard in the tart crust. Coated them with an apricot glaze. He had a pint of ice cream but wondered if he should mention it—if it would be too much, too precious for a first date, apple tart and ice cream. He wanted the dinner to seem simple, spontaneous.

***

When Owen had decided to call Margo, he hoped it wasn't professionally improper. He pushed his doubts aside and pretended himself into a confident guy who did stuff like this all the time. He thought, *BRAVADO*, in all caps. "Hello Margo!" he said, talking in exclamation points. "I thought I'd make you dinner? How about Saturday? I'll pick you up! Don't worry about a thing! My treat for embarrassing you there at the opening in front of Dirk!"

Later, Owen wondered if Margo even knew who was calling. If maybe she thought he was some other, stronger, more interesting man who'd embarrassed her at the art opening. She had asked for time to think about it, but then called back to say yes, adding that she was capable of driving herself. Asked for the directions twice. Everything a little more serious than Owen had imagined. But still. Margo agreed to come for dinner with her hair and her wryness. Owen hadn't imagined such a thing possible, but there, it had popped to life.

***

Prompt, Margo looked more relaxed than Owen had thought possible. Her hair pulled back with a thin barrette, just a tuck at her forehead. Snug-fitting jeans and a slate blue silk shirt. The same black clogs she had worn at the exhibition. A thin gold chain at her neck. Owen opened the door, and her brow unfurrowed.

"This is the right place? It's microscopic. You live in a room," she said, tentatively taking a glance inside.

"Quality over quantity," Owen said. "I don't like stuff, so I've eliminated the option."

Margo walked in, made a brief circle. "It is cozy," she said. "It's well done, too. Nice decisions, Owen." She fingered the stand-up lamp's shade, touched the tapestry throw pillow on the couch. Margo turned to him then and smiled. It was, Owen felt, the first time she had actually looked at him, and then it struck him that she had to be claustrophobically lonely. In order to say yes to his invitation, out of the blue. She must. *There must* . . . he couldn't finish his thought. She smiled at him, and he smiled back. "Let me show you the kitchen," he said. "Walk slowly and you won't knock anything over, but rest assured if you do knock something over it won't be the first time it has met the floor."

She held out a bottle of red wine. "I hope this works with what you're making. I just wasn't sure what to bring." Owen took the bottle. It was a fine wine, and they would drink that bottle as well as another and then Owen would open up the Porto his coworker had brought back for him from Portugal. He'd open up the Porto and serve Margo the tart with ice cream without even asking. They'd sit in the little kitchen and not knock over a thing. Margo would soften and smile and a wisp of hair would stray from her barrette. Owen was sure he could see what she looked like as a little girl, although he didn't tell her that. He didn't want to worry her. He could tell Margo carried worry with her nearly everywhere she went.

They were tipsy by the time they moved to the living room. Margo sat on the floor looking at art books, paging slowly through. She'd taken off her clogs, revealing bright purple-and-yellow striped socks, thin stripes (*tasteful*, Owen thought) running horizontally around her feet up her ankles. That she owned these socks was surely a sign, Owen thought, that she would be okay. A good sign.

Owen had worried, throughout his life, that he served as a bad luck charm. His father's death. His mother left adrift to raise him. From a very young age he looked for signs that people were going to be okay around him. Thc world always seemed to be faltering, even if that wasn't necessarily true. He wanted people to survive him, to stay alive. He searched for clues. The socks seemed to suggest that Margo had something inside her to battle the unluckiness in him. And without thinking and because he couldn't really maintain overthinking at this stage in his port drinking, he said, "Do you think you're a lucky person, Margo?"

Margo looked up quickly from the Basquiat catalog she'd been thumbing through. "What do you mean?" she said, her brown eyes suspicious, like it was the beginning of a pickup line.

Owen fumbled, looked into his nearly empty glass, the thick red port swishing and settling flat. "Oh, nothing, you know, I just wondered if . . . It's just important for me to know."

Margo clearly didn't believe in luck. In superstitions, in charms or rituals. Owen could tell. In this, they were worlds apart. Owen's entire existence strung together deals and bets with the universe, systems and plans to make sure all could go well. Owen's entire life was based on luck—good and bad. It's what tied him to everything else.

"I have been lucky," Margo said. She folded shut the book and carefully set it on the rug beside her. She leaned back against the armchair. "Will that satisfy your concern?"

Owen said yes, that would do.

She tipped her watch face toward the light, moving efficiently even in her near drunkenness, even though Owen doubted she could see the tiny numbers in the dim light. Margo looked at Owen.

They both said coffee at the same time as if strategizing on how to make this first date a successful one. Owen made coffee, poured it into deep blue mugs. He asked Margo if she'd like to go for a walk. With their hands occupied by coffee there was no danger of decisions, of whether he should try to hold her hand or let his arms swing free. They held their coffee cups, walked through the quiet blocks near his house. It was near midterm, and students were buckling down behind all the front doors—they could feel it.

Owen walked up to the big house and onto the wide, sprawling porch. "We share the porch," Owen said. "Worked that out years ago." They sat on the rattan couch someone had plopped there; no one remembered when. They drank their coffee, and Owen said, "I mean, like, are you happy? I was just wondering, because sometimes I feel like I'm missing something, like a part is gone, you know? I wondered if that made sense to you?"

"Dirk sent me here this evening," Margot said, rubbing her finger along the edge of her mug. "You deserve to know that. The museum is my life. I feel lucky to have a job there. He thought the idea of a date with you would be fun. Am I unhappy? I have no idea."

"What," Owen said. "Dirk's your matchmaker?"

"Ah, he overextends his influence in every aspect of my life," Margot said. "I didn't intend to have such a good time. I didn't intend to enjoy your company."

Owen pulled his notebook from his back pocket, the little pencil from his front pocket. As Margot continued to apologize for her callous behavior, Owen drew her hair, her profile. He sketched by porchlight as a few cars made their way past the big house, headlights spotlighting them and moving on. He sketched quickly, with purpose. A decent portrait.

He wondered if the date was finally a manifestation of a communication from his dead father after all these years. A joke? His mother always said his father had such a strange sense of humor. Was it because he had worn the red handkerchief, a red light to green-light this evening? Dirk's revenge. Owen didn't know. He'd never know.

"We'll have to sit here until you're sober enough to drive," Owen said. "Before this. Before what you just said, I was thinking maybe you'd stay over. We'd go to breakfast in the morning."

"Yeah, no," Margot said.

Margot didn't feel a need to protect or coddle Owen, and he could feel that, sitting on the couch beside her. Maybe it was a breakthrough, this messed-up joke of an actually good bad date, the world such a confusing place. Owen knew his mother would boycott the museum after he told her this story. And Caroline would take him off the museum campaign and give it to someone else, probably Kendra. Owen would keep the portrait, sometimes running across it in his pile of sketches as time moved forward. He'd never see Margot again, somehow. As if she had been a figment of his imagination, a snap of memory.

Later that night, after he watched Margo's brake lights blip red at the stop sign down the block, Owen crawled up into his loft, confused and curious. He slept into the late hours of the morning with the red silk handkerchief tucked neatly under his pillow.

When he woke, Owen propped himself up in bed, smoothed the

sheets around him, gazed out at the hazy yellow horizon framing his town. A shaky new start of a day. *Margo*, he thought. *What in the hell?* And just like that, a memory of Owen's father dislodged into his brain, blinking like a faulty electric connection. The first memory he'd ever had that wasn't fabricated from a photo or from his mother's stories. It was his: A thick hand on a red tricycle handlebar, big fatherly fingers guiding Owen along a sidewalk. Red bike. Green leaves. Little kid knees pumping the pedals. The person behind the hand, his father, laughed and laughed, deep from his stomach, laughing at his own jokes, pushing the bike forward as Owen pedaled to keep up. Then the connection cut out, done.

Owen reached to open the window, shifting a thick black handle to let the frame swivel. He fidgeted with the screen, got it free, set it aside. He wanted to face this day head on. A cool, colorless breeze floated in. Owen pulled the handkerchief out from under his pillow. He held it by its silky edge. It flashed a red heartbeat, alive. Owen flung it, let it go, out into the world. It wavered like a hand and then the breeze puffed it full. It pulsed once, rose up over his roof. Gone.

ARNIE AND THE BEAR THINK ABOUT RISK

The bear thinks there's something so sweetly romantic about a paper cup of coffee held nonchalantly by a woman in a conversation on the street corner. The bear can't help himself. He's drawn to these intersections. The light turns red, the woman waits with her friend to cross, a nip in the air, her breath streaming out in a little foggy wisp before she takes another sip, mittens on her hands. The woman's knitted cap is pulled down over her long hair. The light turns green, and she walks, purposeful strides, purple tights. The bear trundles after her into the crosswalk.

He continues on to his third-floor office on the edge of downtown. The coffee machine is nearly always broken, so he brings his own small thermos from home. It's one of his morning pleasures, to uncap the thermos and pour the coffee into his pottery mug. The coffee smell intensifies in that first moment of uncapping, and he feels something very close to love, watching the steam rise. The bear shuts his eyes for a moment and remembers blueberries and sunny skies. Forests of deciduous trees. He shuts the door, so happy to have the solid click of the latch in its notch. He reads his two morning newspapers. He sends some relevant links to his staff. And then the mug is empty and his regular day is before him, sloped like a nice hill that runs into 5 p.m.'s open arms. He straightens his tie and prepares the files for the afternoon meeting, shuffling papers with his big bear paws.

***

Yesterday, Arnold Elmer was in a mood. He sulked by the copier and then left the office right at five, head down, without saying goodbye. Today, the bear tries to think of something to congratulate Arnold for in the upcoming meeting—something to perk him up. A witty anecdote or a helpful gesture. The bear is pretty sure Arnold was the one to lug in the giant Costco container of peanut butter filled pretzels that everyone loves, for instance.

Just then Arnold himself knocks on the door, his soft tapping distinct from most everyone else, who tends to barge in and then ask the bear if they're interrupting.

"Come on in, mister," the bear says, putting on his best bear face so his good morning can slide over a little into Arnold, if Arnold is interested. "How you doing this fine day?" he says, gesturing to the comfy chair in the corner.

"I'm fantastic," Arnold says with no inflection. "Always fantastic. You know that." He dumps himself into the uncomfortable chair in front of the bear's desk. Arnold looks longingly at the bear's thermos for a sec, and then out the window as if the bear had called him in for a chat instead of Arnold initiating this whole sit-down situation.

"And so," the bear says, swinging his big furry arms out to encompass the room, "you've come to me for . . . ?"

Arnold puts his hands together like a little church steeple and sighs. "Honestly, I'm bored," he says. "I'm not fantastic. That's just a thing I've taught myself to say." Arnold looks longingly at the bear's mug, which is now empty, but still thick and inviting. Ceramic pottery the bear made at the community college years ago. "Did you know people used to call me Arnie? I used to have this group of friends. We had so much fun, camping and traveling together in our twenties." Arnold leans forward, straining his tied-in neck against his buttoned shirt. "Did you know I used to be in a band, for Christ's sake? Like, a pretty decent band."

The bear did not know this about Arnold, which is strange, he thinks, because they've actually gone out for their fair share of drinks, commiserating over sports and dates more times than he can remember. Even though the bear is technically Arnold's boss, it has never felt that way for the bear. "You were in a band?" the bear says. He really wishes he had more coffee in his thermos and thinks again about the woman's inviting to-go cup and how he could get his own after they finish talking here. Scoot out before the sales meeting, maybe.

"I knew you were going to fixate on that," Arnold says. "Yes, a kind of acoustic alt-rock/country kind of thing. We were pretty decent." Arnold taps his knee a little—maybe tapping out an old tune he used to play, sing.

"You mentioned that. Being pretty decent. Cool. What instrument did you play? You were the drummer, weren't you? You're a Ringo kind of guy, right?" The bear picks up the baseball he keeps balanced on a tiny podium on his desk. He likes to squeeze it to see if he can crush it flat. He never does, but its hard surface is helpful in keeping him centered. Squeeze.

Arnold sighs. "I have become a Ringo kind of guy, yes, but back then, man, I was Lennon. Lennon!" For a moment he makes intense eye contact, and the bear can almost see it—Arnie, lead vocals and rhythm guitar.

They both stare at each other for a while—the kind of silence that feels like standing on the edge of a cliff. Squeeze.

"And so," the bear says.

"And so, I think I'd like to take a leave of absence," Arnold says. "I want to get back to being, you know, Arnie again."

"Okay. Okay. Starting when?" The bear flips open his laptop. Here is something he can dig into and facilitate, his best skill. He clicks his calendar front and center. "What. Like a couple weeks to find yourself? Buy a new guitar?"

"Six months should do it," Arnold says.

"That's a lot of time, Arnold," the bear says evenly. "Really too much. Maybe you could work a few part-time remote hours?"

But Arnold isn't budging. The bear sees he's about to lose his best salesperson to an idea—a *new* idea of himself.

Soon Arnold shakes the bear's paw and heads down the hall to his own office. Tomorrow he'll saunter into the world of his past that doesn't exist anymore but that he'll try to recreate so that he feels like he hasn't really lost himself completely in the corporate world that is, in fact, eating him alive.

What to think of all this, the bear wonders. Such a risky move for Arnold. The bear considers whether he has made any risky moves in his life. He knows, sure, he's a bear working in a managerial level position at a financially solid corporation with a downtown office building. But did he take risks to get here? One thing led to another. He remembers blackberries—pulling the fruit in big swipes from the looping canes into his mouth, like a conveyor belt. The sun, oh man, the sun on his fur. But the bear likes watching people walk around the city, and he likes to spend time at home in his cozy den, reading and petting his small dog, even though it's weird for a bear to own a pet. Sometimes he likes to golf, to lumber from hole to hole, but not usually, and sometimes he likes to cook for pretty women. He genuinely loves to cook for pretty women, and they always really love his dog, Benny.

The bear gathers up his computer and his phone and tilts himself toward the back conference room. Maybe he should learn an instrument, he thinks. Maybe the piano. He could become a middle-aged sensation and then women would love his food for different reasons. But he won't do that. He knows he won't. There are only so many changes one can make in a lifetime.

What would he revisit from his past if he could? Not much. His mom. A den. Rambling through the stream with his brothers, who are all off in Alaska fishing.

Wasn't this the goal? The bear suddenly feels that maybe it's wrong to want such a nice life. Was the plan really for the bear just to exist happily like this forever? One day he'll be old and then who will take care of him? No one. That's who. Maybe it isn't okay to feel okay being alone and content walking the dog.

He knows these feelings are all Arnold's fault.

As he ambles the narrow corridor toward his hardworking staff, minus one, the bear still clutches the baseball. He gives it a good long squeeze. He imagines throwing a fastball, low, right across the middle of home plate. The sweet smell of the cropped field grass, the sun, the crowd's hum. The batter is up and ready. The bear leans back, extending a big furry arm toward the outfield, pulling up his big furry knee. He swivels, and the ball leaves his fingers like a song.

ACKNOWLEDGMENTS

I would like to thank the journals and magazines that originally published many of these stories, some in different form.

Arrowsmith Journal: "Lost in Time"
Atticus Review: "Harry, Secured"
Booth: "Breaking," "Into the Night," and "Arnie and the Bear Think About Risk"
Boudin: "Trench Coat"
Elm Leaves Journal (ELJ): "The Visitor" and "Bear in a Canoe"
Flash Boulevard: "Paradise" and "The Bear Plays Basketball"
Healing Visions (anthology), Matter Press: "Light and Shadow"
The Journal of Compressed Creative Arts: "Winning"
The Laconic: "Squawk" and "Everything Okay" (as "Dinner Rolls")
Los Angeles Review: "Like Love"
The Masters Review: "Woodpeckers Peck to Establish Territory in the Spring"
Mom Egg Review: "Honesty"
Moon City Review: "Like Rain"
Northern Appalachia Review: "Vitamin D," "Berries," "We Need to Talk," and "Chlorophyll and Oxidation"
Puerto del Sol: "Bobby the Bear"
Pithead Chapel: "Scotty, Not Scott"
Western Humanities Review: "Freddy," "Two Bears," "Precession," and "Living"

***

Singular gigantic gratitude goes to The Heinz Endowments, who supported the completion of *I Have Not Considered Consequences* with a 2023 Creative Development Award.

More gratitude to The Greater Pittsburgh Arts Council for an Emergency Funds for Artists grant, which came at the manuscript's conception during the COVID-19 pandemic.

More thanks to the amazing people who have helped carry me through the writing and revising of this book and much more. My fabulous editors Christine Stroud and Hattie Fletcher. The Scrappy Motherfuckers (Sarah Shotland, Hattie Fletcher [again], Joy Katz, Danielle Chiotti, and Brittany Hailer). The Quaker Lake retreat, where many of these stories were drafted (Milena Nigam, Hallie Pritts, Sharla Yates, Lisa Slage Robinson, Bergita Bugarija, and Stephanie Vega). The Flick family, especially Don and Shirley Flick. Mike Good, Elle Randolph, Beth Kracklauer, Alice Julier, Diane Cecily, Elvira Eichleay, the Friday night kitchen hoot, the Pymatuning Sailing Club, Hilda Raz, Chauna Craig, Sandy Yannone, Liz Ahl, Karen Shoemaker, Heather Lundine, Guy Capecelatro, Christopher Allen and the *SmokeLong Quarterly* crew, Kati Csoman, Mary Brice, James Simon, John Fleenor, Rachel Klipa & Shiftworks Creative Corps, Bubby, and Jo-Jo.

I'm grateful for David Pohl's generous offer to create the cover art for this book, which I love. Thanks to Kinsley Stocum for the design that brought it all together. A selection of Sharon Harper's artwork inspired the story "Breaking," and that story is dedicated to Steve Pesci. Additional thanks to Joy Katz for the tennis insights incorporated into "In Search Of."

More thanks and gratitude go to the journal editors who supported my work by publishing some of these stories in advance of this publication: Vlad Beu, Randall Brown, Michael Czyzniejewski, Damian Dressick, John Fulton, Maura Hehir, Sophia Ihlefeld, Kim Magowan, Tara Masih, Michael Mejia, Cole Meyer, Michelle Ross, Robert Stapleton, and Francine Witte.

Special, special thanks to the bear, whoever you are, wherever you came from.

As always, so much love to Rick Schweikert for all he does to keep my heart on track.

NEW & FORTHCOMING FROM AUTUMN HOUSE PRESS

The Worried Well by Anthony Immergluck
Winner of the 2024 Autumn House Rising Writer Prize, selected by Eduardo C. Corral

Rodeo by Sunni Brown Wilkinson
Winner of the 2024 Donald Justice Poetry Prize, selected by Patricia Smith

Bigger: Essays by Ren Cedar Fuller
Winner of the 2024 Autumn House Nonfiction Prize, selected by Clifford Thompson

The Great Grown-Up Game of Make-Believe by Lauren D. Woods
Winner of the 2024 Autumn House Fiction Prize, selected by Kristen Arnett

self-driving by Betsy Fagin
Winner of the 2024 Autumn House Poetry Prize, selected by Kazim Ali

For our full catalog please visit autumnhouse.org